Here's

(

BOOKS BY GEMMA HALLIDAY

High Heels Mysteries
Spying in High Heels
Killer in High Heels
Undercover in High Heels
Christmas in High Heels
(short story)
Alibi in High Heels
Mayhem in High Heels
Honeymoon in High Heels
(short story)
Sweetheart in High Heels
(short story)
Fearless in High Heels
Danger in High Heels
Homicide in High Heels
Deadly in High Heels

Hollywood Headlines
Mysteries
Hollywood Scandals
Hollywood Secrets
Hollywood Confessions
Twelve's Drummer Dying
(holiday short story)

Jamie Bond Mysteries
Unbreakable Bond
Secret Bond
Bond Bombshell
(short story)
Lethal Bond

Tahoe Tessie Mysteries
Luck Be A Lady
Hey Big Spender
(coming soon)

Young Adult Books
Deadly Cool
Social Suicide

Other Works
Play Nice
Viva Las Vegas
A High Heels Haunting
Watching You (short story)
Confessions of a Bombshell
Bandit (short story)

BOOKS BY JENNIFER FISCHETTO

Disturbia Diaries Mysteries
I Spy Dead People
We Are the Weirdos

Jamie Bond Mysteries
Unbreakable Bond
Secret Bond
Lethal Bond

LETHAL BOND

GEMMA HALLIDAY

AND

JENNIFER FISCHETTO

To my kids—*always*

~ Jennifer

For my Bond Girls, Michelle & Susan. You ladies rock.

~ Gemma

CHAPTER ONE

———

I popped another Flamin' Hot Cheeto into my mouth and zoomed in on the office building across the street with my sleek, new binoculars. Waterproof, image stabilizing, and compact enough to toss into my bag, they may have set me back a couple months worth of after-hour cocktails, but since they were a business expense, I could write them off. Plus, they were necessary in my line of work. Up there with my Glock and spy cam brooch.

Luckily for me the building was all concrete and glass. The windows ran from floor to ceiling, and the blinds were up, which meant I had a perfect interior view from my car. Pretty sweet.

I focused on the office dead center on the third floor and waited for another glimpse of the couple. They'd walked off a few minutes ago, and I hoped they'd return before I turned into a pumpkin. My phone said the hour was inching in on eleven. They were busy bees, working overtime, especially on a Sunday night. Didn't anyone take a day off anymore?

Then again, here I was on a stakeout. But my crazy hours were demanded by my cases.

I reached for another deep-fried, smothered in fake cheese, kernel of deliciousness when he walked back into my view. Brushing my fingers off on a napkin on my leg, I steadied the binoculars.

He read a sheet of paper and sat on the edge of his desk. His navy tie was unknotted, the collar of his white button-down loosened, and his blonde hair tousled, as if he'd run his fingers through it one too many times.

Or maybe *she* had.

The tall, leggy brunette strutted up to him like a cat in heat. She said something that made him look up and grin. Too bad I'd never learned how to read lips. She trailed her finger down his forearm and leaned forward so he had a perfect view of her cleavage. Her boobs nearly popped out of her tight, white blouse. She flaunted her sexuality like a flashing, neon sign. The words "subtle" and "coy" obviously weren't a part of her personal dictionary.

He tilted his head back and laughed. It must've been nice to get that reaction from him.

I would know, considering we'd had a brief thing not even a couple of weeks ago.

Assistant District Attorney Aiden Prince was usually all business. It was one of the reasons it had taken him way too long to lean in for our first kiss. The other reason had been his dead wife. One minute things were hot and heavy in my apartment, and the next night he'd dumped me on my front steps. Okay, so dumped was too harsh a word. He'd said he *wanted* to see me but that he just wasn't ready to move on yet. That he felt guilty about dating when his wife had died of breast cancer only a year ago.

I understood. Mostly. Besides, what could I have done? Wrestled him to the ground and demanded he date me? It was hard to compete with a ghost. It hadn't meant he and I were over, but we hadn't been hot and heavy since. More like lukewarm and feather light.

And if his reasoning was true, what the hell was going on in his office right now?

Miranda Valens, Aiden's second chair in the courtroom, flipped her hair off her shoulders in that seductive shampoo commercial sorta way. This woman had cliché flirting 101 perfected. How predictable.

If Aiden fell for that…

He stood up and walked around his desk, settling into his chair—farther away from her.

"Ha," I shouted then glanced around to make sure no one heard me.

We may have been heading toward the tail end of summer, but it was still too warm to sit cooped up. I was smart enough to have the top up on my cherry red Roadster convertible, but the windows were down. The last thing I needed was a concerned person to spot me spying and calling the cops.

When I was certain no one was around, I brought the binoculars back up again.

Miranda had walked around to the other side of his desk and perched herself on the edge. She placed a stockinged foot on his chair, beside his thigh, and arched her back.

I attempted to roll my eyes, but it was a hard feat with the binoculars pressed against them.

Aiden stayed seated and still. He didn't lean forward, touch her, or do anything that suggested he was interested. Not that it mattered. This wasn't why I was spying. If he was suddenly ready to move on, and it was with someone else, that was none of my business. I'd be happy for him.

Eventually.

No, tonight was about a tip I'd received last week that there was corruption in the D.A.'s office. Someone fixing cases for compensation that far outweighed the usual civil servant pension. My intention was to find out how far it extended before it reached Aiden. So every night I've been here, keeping my eye on things, hoping I'd learn who the dirty lawyer was before Aiden got burned.

My cell rang. I reached for it and glanced at the ID. Danny Flynn.

If my relationship with Aiden was complicated, throwing Danny into the mix brought the meaning of the word to a whole new level.

"You were just released from the hospital. Isn't it past your bedtime?" I said into the phone.

His deep, infectious laughter filled my ear. "And hello to you too."

I'd known Danny since I was a gangly fourteen-year-old, when I'd first started posing in bikinis and haute couture for DeLine Model Agency. He was the first photographer who'd filmed me and the only one who'd used a combo of over-the-top comical flirtations and brotherly love to make me feel at ease.

But some time in the last couple of months the brotherly love had morphed into something else. It wasn't what I'd call *love* love, but I wasn't entirely sure what I felt where Danny was concerned anymore. Something bordering on affection with just the slightest hint of lust.

"The docs say I can't drive for another week, but they want me to go to therapy. Do they expect me to walk?" he asked.

"How dare they. Maybe they expect you to take the bus." I knew what he was after, but teasing him felt like a great distraction. I smiled and lowered the binoculars.

He gasped. "Los Angeles has public transportation?"

"Shocker, right?" Clearly we were both practicing our sarcasm.

"The appointments are from three to four. I have rides there. Mrs. Rosenbaum is dropping me off every day this week."

Mrs. Rosenbaum was his next door neighbor who baked him Bundt cakes and asked him to sit in on weekly games of pinochle when one of her other fond-of-baking, retired friends couldn't make it. She treated Danny like a son, always looking out for him and offering unsolicited advice.

"But she can't pick me up," he continued. "She volunteers at the library."

She also loved books and was always dropping off ones she thought Danny would enjoy from her massive collection. I don't think I ever saw him read a book, but he always graciously had it sitting on his coffee table. The bookmark never moving.

He cleared his throat. "I know you're busy with cheaters and liars and all, but maybe you can find time in your busy schedule to pick up a poor, injured man?"

"Flynn, is that your way of asking for a favor?"

"Pathetic?"

I bit my lip to keep from laughing. "Yes."

"You wound me deeper than a bullet, Bond." While his tone was joking, the words hit just a little too close to home. He had, in fact, taken a bullet. For my father no less. To say I owed him one was a massive understatement.

"Of course I'll pick you up," I promised.

"Great." I could practically see his grin. He'd known all along I'd cave. "Where are you?" he asked. "It sounds like you're outside."

I glanced at a car turning at the intersection. "I'm on a stakeout." One I seriously needed to get back to.

"It's safe, right?"

I smiled at how protective he sounded. "Of course. Besides, I'm almost done. And you need sleep to heal. Good night."

"'Night, Jamie." Something about the way he said my name made my insides go warm and liquid, like a shot of Cuervo.

I clicked off the call and reassumed my position.

Aiden was still seated, and Miranda still trying everything in her arsenal to get closer to him. She leaned forward so much, she was practically in his lap.

My cheeks grew warm, and I suddenly felt weird and uncomfortable. And way too voyeuristic. I was keeping an eye on corruption, not Aiden's potential love life. And clearly the only person with "corrupting" on their minds tonight was Miranda.

I tossed the binoculars onto the passenger seat, feeling an "ick" settle in my stomach that had nothing to do with my Cheeto dinner. I was not a jealous woman. I didn't spy on potential boyfriends. Well, unless it involved payment, but I was not a client. No, this was supposed to be about helping Aiden. Nothing more.

Then why did I feel like I needed a shower?

I turned my key in the ignition and headed home.

* * *

The next morning I stepped into the Bond Agency groggy and in need of a caffeinated I.V. drip. When I'd gotten home the night before, I hadn't been able to force my mind to settle down enough for sleep. I'd tossed and turned for two hours before my weary body won out. This morning it was still tired and fought me every step of the way.

Maya Alexander, former March Playmate and current office manager extraordinaire, greeted me with a Caramel Macchiato.

God, I loved this woman.

"Morning, boss," she said in her chipper, morning-person tone.

I took a scalding sip while she grabbed her tablet and followed me to my office. We were in the process of turning the agency over from paper to digital, unbeknownst to my father, Derek—founder of the Bond Agency.

Sam was waiting, seated cross-legged in one of the chairs facing my desk. While she flipped through the latest fashion magazine, her top leg bounced. An adorable, black with gold accents, open-toed, high-heeled mule balanced precariously on her toes.

"Are you waiting for me?" I asked, which in two-second hindsight was pretty obvious.

She glanced to Maya and waved a hand. "It can wait."

Samantha Cross, fellow former cover model, an associate, and our weapons specialist, grew up as a military brat, living all over the country. She knew how to handle a man as smoothly as an automatic. The one thing she didn't handle well was having to wait. You'd think being a single mom to a growing boy would've taught her this over the years, but not so much. And that leg bouncing suggested there was something she needed to say.

Maya cleared her throat. "Jamie, Mrs. Griffin is coming in so you can hand over the proof on her husband."

Ah, yes, the infamous panty stealer.

As if it wasn't heartbreaking enough that I'd caught and filmed Mr. Griffin cheating on his wife with a bartender downtown, her yoga instructor, *and* her sister, I'd also caught him breaking into seven women's homes to steal their underwear. Seven. I had no idea if he knew them or not, and I didn't want to know. That man needed a shrink and a really good divorce attorney, although I was rooting for the wife to have a better one. I was thrilled this case was over.

"You also have lunch with Derek," Maya said, interrupting my thoughts of the Panty Prowler.

I tried not to sigh too heavily. A part of me felt obligated to endure thirty minutes of my father talking with his mouth full because this was his agency. I'd taken it over three years ago after he'd been shot and his doctor had forbidden stress. Then again, the other part of me, the one still nursing a grudge that, among other parental missteps, the man had named me *James* Bond, wished he'd lose my number.

But he was my dad, and it was a free lunch.

"There's also a new case coming in," Maya continued. "You're meeting with Mrs. Livingston this afternoon."

"What's her story?" I asked, perching on the edge of my desk.

Maya grinned. "She and her husband have an open marriage."

Sam raised her brows. The leg stopped bouncing.

Maya glanced at her notes. "She's worried that her husband might be secretly monogamous. And she doesn't want that. She said, and I quote, 'the fact that we are both with other people is what makes the relationship work.' End quote. She's hiring you to find out if he's not cheating."

Well that was a first.

Maya handed over my itinerary, and I checked to make sure there was a gap in my day to pick up Danny. Luckily, there was. "Thanks, Maya."

When she walked out, I stared at Sam. "What's going on?"

She glanced over her shoulder, as if making sure no one else was listening, and leaned forward.

Butterflies swarmed my stomach. This had to be big. My girls weren't usually secret keepers. They were pretty transparent about most things.

"Something is up with Caleigh."

I frowned, not even a little bit sure what she referred to. "In what way?"

Sam rose and cocked her head toward my door. "Come on. I'll show you."

I grabbed my coffee and followed her out across the waiting area to Caleigh's office.

Before even stepping inside, I noticed a full-length mirror propped up against a wall. That wasn't there yesterday. Was Caleigh having another new-date fashion crisis?

Caleigh Presley rounded out our quartet. Another investigator and retired model, she told everyone she met that she was the distant cousin of Elvis. Smart, sexy, and southern,

Caleigh brought a bubbly touch to the agency. As well as the skills of a professional computer hacker. She was Yin to Sam's Yang, in not only personality but looks too. Caleigh was blonde, naturally pale with big blue eyes, and had the temperament of cotton candy—light and sweet. Whereas, Sam was all long legs, mocha-colored skin, and dark curls wound as tight as her aim.

When I stepped inside Caleigh's office, I sucked in a breath.

She was wearing a wedding gown. Victorian lace, high collar, pearl bodice, puffed shoulders, long sleeves, blinding white, floor-length with a train, and a full veil, wedding gown.

I glanced to Sam, who pressed her lips together and shrugged. I couldn't speak for a moment. Had Caleigh been dating someone and forgot to tell us?

"Cal, what's going on?" The words finally made it out of my mouth.

"Need a couple of bridesmaids?" Sam asked.

Caleigh puckered her brows at Sam then shook her head. "This isn't real. My God, you'd be the first to know if I was dating anyone serious enough to marry."

Sam and I let out a collective breath.

"Then what's with the dress?" I asked.

Caleigh stared at me straight in the eye. "Because Daddy's coming, of course."

Of course.

"And you plan on marrying him?" Sam asked.

Caleigh shook her head, oblivious to the ribbing Sam was doing at her expense.

"I kinda told him I was getting married."

Sam snorted. I covered my mouth to hold back a laugh.

"Oh, honey," I said, "what on Earth possessed you to do that?"

Caleigh plopped into her desk chair. "He's always going on and on about how I need to settle down and do the housewife thing, have babies, you know. With Mama gone, he's been pushing my sisters and me harder than usual. So, to get him off my back, I blurted out, 'Surprise, I'm engaged.'"

Surprise indeed.

She held out her left hand and showed us a ring with a rock as big as my thumb. "It's not real. Just a two-carat, marquis Cubic Zirconia. I bought it off Amazon and had it shipped overnight. Isn't it beautiful though?"

While she admired her fake diamond, Sam and I exchanged looks again. Sam was right. Caleigh's behavior was beyond any she normally displayed.

"This was my Mama's wedding dress, when she married Daddy. He sent it up so I could wear it, like I always said I wanted to." She sniffled. "Wasn't that sweet of him?"

I stepped closer. "It is, but how long do you think you can keep up this pretense?"

Caleigh shrugged. "I was kinda hoping forever."

"Just tell him the truth," Sam said.

Her eyes widened. She looked like Sam had raised a palm and struck her. "Are you kidding? There's no way I am going back on anything. He'd never let me forget it. Oh no, I'd endure phone call after phone call about how much I pained and embarrassed him. I'm sure he's told everyone we know from back home. That man is as stubborn as they come." Her tone had hardened.

I thought of Derek. I knew exactly what it was like to have an interfering father who thought he knew best. About everything.

Sam groaned. Her father was Command Sergeant Major Cross. She also knew it all too well.

"How can we help?" I asked.

Caleigh wiped the corners of her eyes. "Right now, he's on his way to visit my sister in Florida. He'll be here in L.A. the week after. He's staying for five days and four nights, so I only have to pretend for less than a week. It can't be that hard, right?"

In theory, maybe not, except… "What happens when he wants to meet his future son-in-law?" I asked, hoping she'd realize how insane this was and figure out a way to call it off. There was no reason her father would hold it against her if she and her mysterious fiancé suddenly called their engagement off.

"Well, that's where I'm planning on begging someone to play along."

"Someone?" Sam asked. "Like a stranger off the street?"

Caleigh scrunched up her face. "No, I asked Danny."

Sam chuckled.

I froze. "My Danny?" Well, not that he was *mine* exactly but...

"Why is that funny?" Caleigh asked Sam, ignoring me.

Sam glanced to me. I wasn't sure if she was looking for help or if she heard me. Either way, she faced Caleigh and frowned. "Because this is crazy. You can't pretend to be engaged."

Caleigh stood and went back to admiring herself in the mirror. "Why not? People do it all the time."

"What people? The ones on soap operas? They don't exactly count. Besides you can't do it with...him."

From the mirror's reflection, I watched Sam cock her head toward me.

It took Caleigh a moment. Then she turned and grabbed my arms. "Oh my goodness, I didn't mean to upset you. I mean, I didn't even really mean to ask Danny. That afternoon I visited him in the hospital, I'd just heard from Daddy, and I was rambling, and the idea popped into my head."

Her eyes widened when she said, "popped," all animated-like. She let me go and took a step back. "If it makes you uncomfortable, well, I'll just find someone else."

When she stopped speaking, she gasped for air.

Sam had scrunched up her mouth and squinted, as if she was anticipating my response and assumed it would entail yelling or crying or something less than pleasant. Which surprised me considering she knew me well enough to know I did neither of the two. Usually.

"It's fine," I said. And it was. Danny and I were just friends. Like Aiden, Danny could see, pretend with, and date whomever he wanted.

"You're sure?" Sam asked, giving me her best get real look.

"Positive." And I was. Even if the odd twist in the pit of my stomach at the thought of Danny cozying up to my hottest employee as her fiancé wasn't as convinced.

* * *

The rest of my morning after Caleigh's fake engagement announcement entailed listening to Mrs. Griffin ranted about her adulterous thief of a future ex-husband. She muttered words like "divorce, public humiliation, and Lorena Bobbitt." Then she dialed the police, ratted on her husband's panty heists, paid her bill, and walked out. Hopefully I'd never see either of them again, but I also hoped I wouldn't find out on the evening news that Mr. Griffin was missing his family jewels.

After ridding myself of one pain in the butt, I went to meet the other—Derek. By the time I pulled up to the greasy roadside taco joint, he was already in line. I grimaced as I joined him. The place was clearly his choice. Definitely not mine. Mine would've included white tablecloths and actual silverware, rather than plastic sporks. Four walls would've been nice too. The fact that there were three people ahead of us and at least eight behind made me feel a bit safer about eating here. But just a bit. I couldn't help but visually inspect the area, looking out for roaches or puppy-sized rodents as Derek greeted me with his usual, "Hey, kid."

It seemed clean, but I still had my doubts.

Derek ordered fish tacos for both of us. Sometimes I hated that he knew me so well. Normally I'd make a stink about a guy ordering for me without asking, but the fact was, they were my fave. Plus, I was starved and had to admit everything smelled great.

We grabbed our plates of tacos, refried beans, and rice with a bottles of water (for me) and a Corona (for Derek, whose philosophy in life centered around it always being five o'clock somewhere) and headed to an empty picnic table.

"Since when do you eat fish?" I asked, sliding onto the seat. I would've assumed he'd order the beef, or if they had it, roasted pig slathered in barbecue sauce.

"I've been trying to make some changes. Give the old ticker a fighting chance."

I eyed him suspiciously. "Hmmm."

He had dark circles under his eyes. He wasn't sleeping. I tried not to imagine what activities or sexual athletics could be keeping him awake. If this was three years ago or even three months, I'd assume he was worried about my taking over the business, but we were past that now.

I hoped.

I bit into my first taco. A mixture of mild fish, lemon, red cabbage, a hint of mayo, and saltiness exploded in my mouth. Oh wow, this was good.

I must've made my everything-is-right-with-the-world face because Derek grinned and nodded. "I knew you'd like it. I know my food."

I scoffed. Loudly. He was far from a foodie. While the tacos were great, he also used this same enthusiasm when ordering a Big Mac value meal at McDonalds.

"What?" he asked, looking mildly offended.

"This is your idea of fancy dining. Just because the meal tastes great doesn't mean I want to share it with flies and mosquitoes."

He waved a hand at my words. "Pfft. What's wrong with it? You don't need a reservation. There's no wait. You can usually get a table right away."

There were ten tables total. One was empty at the moment.

"José, the owner and cook, is always polite, and if you're one of his favorites, he gives you extra beans."

I glanced to Derek's plate. Sure enough, his scoop of mashed gook was higher than mine. "So you'll be extra gassy? That's wonderful."

Derek narrowed his eyes. "And the food is delicious."

I nodded. "I'll give you the delicious part."

We went about stuffing our bellies in silence. Derek shoveled the refried beans into his mouth as if he was in a race. A glob of it landed on his white Polo shirt. He scraped it off and ignored the stain it left behind. He wasn't a total slob. He may not have always noticed toast crumbs on his kitchenette counter, or a coffee spoon stain, but he always showered and laundered and generally took enough care with his appearance to keep the baby boomer women of L.A. county swooning over his charm. But I knew that shirt would end up without pre-cleaners, and next time he wore it, he wouldn't even notice that brown spot.

About half way through my second taco, I stopped searching for signs of an expired health inspection and managed to calm down enough to enjoy my meal.

Then Derek cleared his throat. "So, listen, I need a favor."

I sighed around a mouthful. "I knew a free lunch was too good to be true."

He shook his head. "Don't be like that. This is quality father-daughter time."

I refrained from eye rolling. "If you say so. What do you want?"

"I'm heading out of town for a couple of days. No big deal, but I need you to cover for me."

I paused, narrowing my eyes. "Cover what?"

He shrugged, feigning nonchalance. "Elaine wanted to know where I was going."

"And?"

"And I kinda don't want her knowing."

I shook my head, giving him my best I-can't-believe-*your*-the-parent-and-*I'm*-the-child look. Elaine was Derek's girlfriend, though he wouldn't actually use those commitment-worthy words. But they'd been seeing one another steadily for a couple of months, which was like a lifetime in old man-whore years.

"I told her it had to do with you," he explained. "An infidelity case you're working on."

Since that's all we worked on it was a safe lie. Well, all Derek knew about, at least. What I did privately at the ADA's office was none of his concern. Derek was only interested in what brought in the cash.

"So what's the catch?" I asked.

He took a gulp of beer. "I'm not sure she believed me, so I want you to back me up and keep an eye on her while I'm gone."

Keep an eye on her? What was she, five?

"Seriously? I'm not lying to Elaine so you can run off with some other woman."

He slammed his bottle on the table. "I'm not cheating on Elaine."

That surprised me coming from Derek. The world "cheating" implied a relationship. "So what are you doing?"

"It's…personal. Look, just take care of Elaine for me, okay?"

"She's a grown woman, Derek."

"That doesn't mean she won't need a little handholding."

I narrowed my eyes. "Why? Is something wrong with her?"

He shook his head. "No, look, it's complicated."

I raised a brow, not agreeing to anything until I understood at least a sliver of what he was yammering about.

"She likes me."

This man couldn't tell a story correctly if it was written down word-for-word.

When I still didn't comment, he painfully sighed. "You know. She may be getting attached."

Suddenly it clicked. "Oh, you mean she's fallen in love with you, and you don't want her doing something stupid. Like getting pissed and retaliating by cheating on you?"

And he'd know all about unfaithfulness. Not because of his own habits. Derek liked women. A lot of them. But keeping it casual meant never having to say, "I love you" or "There's someone else." No. He knew because he'd been the Bond Agency for years. While I was posing in bikinis on the French Riviera, he was sitting on a stakeout in his Bonneville, eating a sausage and pepper sub with extra onions, watching some old geezer get it up.

Derek ran a hand across his chin, knocking a grain of rice off his mouth and onto the table. "No worries. She's the faithful kind."

Which suggested he'd be worried if she wasn't. What was happening to dear ol' Dad?

"So, will you do it? Help me out?" His eyes begged.

This whole thing reeked—or maybe that was the Dumpster on the other side of the lot. I didn't know Elaine well, but she seemed like an okay women, not deserving of lies and infidelity. On the up side, however, the old man would be out of my hair for two full days. That was dancing in the streets naked worthy.

I sipped my water. "Fine." Why did I already feel I was going to live to regret this?

CHAPTER TWO

———

Mrs. Katherine Livingston sat before my desk in a modest, gray, knee-length, A-line skirt, a white blouse with a ruffled collar, and brown penny loafers. Her brown hair was pulled back into a loose bun, and she wore no makeup, not even ChapStick. Her hands were folded on top of her brown, leather purse, which sat squarely in the center of her lap. She was the epitome of poise and restraint. And not exactly what I thought a swinger would look like.

"How can I help you, Mrs. Livingston?" I found that asking clients why they were here, even though they'd already told Maya, was a great way to feel them out, hear the words she chose to describe her marriage. This job may have included spy gear, stakeouts, and skimpy outfits during some undercover work, but the biggest part of it was pure psychology. You had to know what the client truly wanted and how to finesse as well.

She tucked a fallen strand of hair behind her ear. "Please call me Kate. My husband, Stuart, and I have an arrangement. An open marriage."

When I didn't blink or gasp or whatever she expected, she continued, "Lately things are different. I don't think he's been seeing anyone else."

I tried hard not to react, give away some telltale sign that this was all new to me. It was usually at this point in the conversation that I'd think about how the wife was always the first to know when something was wrong in her marriage. In the past three years, I never assumed that "wrong" would be a faithful husband.

"Why do you feel he's not still abiding by the terms of your marriage?" I asked, amazed I hadn't tripped over my words.

I didn't want to insult her simply because I was unfamiliar with the way things worked.

"He's been home every night." Disgust laced her tone.

That would do it.

"Has anything changed for your husband lately, personally or professionally?"

She stared into space for a moment. "Stuart is a sensitive man. He feels everything rather dearly."

And he was okay with his wife seeing other people? I was having a hard time wrapping my head around it, but it sounded like this arrangement was more her idea than his.

"A couple of months ago he feared lay-offs at his job, but he wasn't let go," she said.

I looked over Maya's notes but couldn't find employment. "What does he do?"

"He's an investment banking analyst."

That was some pretty cash. According to their address, the Livingstons lived in a fairly swanky neighborhood in the hills just south of Studio City.

"His brother, well actually his step-brother, Lyle, has recently gone through a messy divorce. He's spent a couple of nights in our spare room, but it was just until he found his own place. Divorce is common in Stuart's family."

Maybe that was why he agreed to an open marriage.

"Other than some overtime, there hasn't been anything that's caused Stuart extra stress," Kate continued.

She obviously didn't think her husband was hiding anything. But no one was honest one-hundred percent of the time.

She pulled a sheet of paper from her purse and handed it to me. "This is a list of the women he's slept with in the past. Perhaps you can talk to them and find out if he's still seeing any of them. Or maybe they know if there's someone new."

I unfolded the sheet and stared at the computer printed list of names. At the top of the page, in bold and underlined, was the heading: Stuart's Girlfriends. Then below were the names of three women in alphabetical order by last name. Melanie Anderson, Nikki Barnes, and Marguerite Clemens. I couldn't help notice that while their last names were A, B, C, their first were M-N-M. Sometimes the universe doled out humor in the most bizarre ways.

So not only did Kate and Stuart agree to see other people, but they also agreed to tell one another who they were? How very...civilized? Or maybe the word was business-like. Why bother to marry if it wouldn't be monogamous? Did they discuss this arrangement before saying, "I do," or was it years later when they realized they were bored? According to the background check Maya did, they were each in their mid-thirties. Certainly that wasn't old enough to warrant a midlife crisis.

This definitely won an award for the weirdest case, but if Stuart was like all the other husbands we've tailed, getting the goods on him would be easy and fast. And for once we'd have a happy wife walking out of the office.

I plastered a confident smile onto my face. "Don't worry. We're thorough. We'll find out if your husband is a cheat—er, faithful or not."

After Kate left, I handed my notes and the printed list of girlfriends to Maya to put into the file. "Where are Caleigh and Sam?" I asked her.

"Sam's outside, waiting for the UPS guy. He's delivering the new chair for my desk."

Maya'd had some tingling in her hand last week, so we'd ordered her an ergonomic chair. I couldn't afford for her to get carpal tunnel syndrome, and I wasn't just referring to the money. Losing her would be devastating.

"Why is Sam waiting though? Won't he deliver it inside?"

Maya smirked. "Yes, but meeting him at the curb gives her a few minutes alone with him."

I grinned. "Is he cute?"

She let out a slight gasp. "That's right. You usually don't see him. Not only is he hot, but he's got a thing for Sam. Always asking about her. I think he's smitten."

I chuckled. Well that explained it. Sam wasn't as flirty as Caleigh, who saw a potential mate in just about every good-looking man out there—and some not so great looking too. That wasn't to say Caleigh slept around. She just loved love. Sam, on the hand, was more practical, especially with a son. When she found someone she felt worthy of bringing into her life, it meant she was serious. And it had been a long time since I'd met any of her dates.

The phone rang. Maya lifted the receiver and covered the mouthpiece with her palm. "Caleigh's in her office."

I nodded my thanks.

At Caleigh's door, I knocked before entering, even though it was partly open. I didn't want to interrupt another wedding fashion moment.

"Come in," she called out.

I stepped over the threshold and let out a breath. The mirror still leaned against the wall, but the gown, veil, and any signs of pre-wedding prep were gone. Caleigh, dressed in a light blue dress, sat at her desk, but her chair was swiveled toward the window looking out onto the street. Daydreaming about her nuptials?

"You busy?" I asked and sat across from her.

"No. What's up?"

"I just spoke with Mrs. Livingston. The swinger."

Caleigh turned to me, giving her full attention. "Oh yeah? How'd that go?"

"Not exactly how I'd expected." I explained the woman's look, demeanor, and our conversation.

"It really makes you wonder about people, huh?" She looked toward the window again.

"Yes, it does. So I'm thinking you can go with me to visit the girlfriends, and I'll have Sam follow him around. See if there's anyone else he's seeing that the wife doesn't know about."

She gave me a quick smile. "Sounds good. It shouldn't be too hard to get the proof."

* * *

As I entered the physical therapy waiting area an hour later, Danny stepped out from behind double doors. Perfect timing.

He wore cargo shorts and a tee with two fingers in a peace sign that fit perfectly against his toned, 6'2" frame. His hair was light brown, streaked with highlights, not from a salon but the honest to goodness California sunshine, a by-product of the outdoor shoots he often worked. It was tousled now, growing a little long to skim his shoulders, but it suited him. When he noticed me, he smiled wide, the corners of his eyes crinkling in a way that I knew had charmed the pants off many a young swimsuit model.

I ignored the urge to be just a little bit charmed by it myself.

"How'd it go?" I asked.

He rotated his shoulder and only winced once. "Not too bad. I won't be hang gliding any time soon, but it's getting there."

I laughed. "Once you're healed, I'd like to see that happen."

"Oh, don't put it past me, Bond. You don't know everything about me." His smile grew bigger, venturing into the flirtatious zone.

"I know you're going home and will have a beer with lunch—probably Chinese delivery," I stated, doing my best not to flirt back.

He shook his head, the smile never dimming. "Can't drink on pain meds."

Concern filled my chest. "You're still taking them?"

"New script for a mild dosage and only when necessary."

We walked to the exit, stepping around a teenage boy on crutches.

Danny wasn't a pill popper. Pain would have to be bad for him to take anything. But if the new prescription was mild, at least it meant he was healing.

We stepped out into the sunlight, and I directed him toward my car. I'd thankfully managed to find a spot not too far away. "Okay, so no alcohol, but I'm right about the Chinese, huh?"

He chuckled. "Normally, perhaps, but Mrs. Rosenbaum brought over a chicken pot pie earlier. It smells amazing."

That woman knew how to cook. I'd been at his apartment once when she'd stopped by with a huge roasted chicken, potatoes, and carrots. She'd said the chickens had been on sale and she thought of Danny. We'd feasted, and he had enough leftovers for nearly a week.

Danny gave me a sideways wink. "You're at zero for two, James. What's up with that?"

I narrowed my eyes. No one but Derek called me by my legal name. "You sure you're not on drugs now. You're in an awfully good mood."

He shook his head causing several strands of hair to fall into his eyes. It made him look endearing. "Nah, just fresh air, exercise." He paused, his eyes roving my outfit, lingering on the hem of my pencil skirt. "Possibly the company."

I gave him a playful punch in his good should. "Does that really work on girls?"

He shrugged. "Most of them." He grinned at me. "But I have other lines. If you're good, maybe you'll get to hear them."

I snorted loudly to diffuse the sudden heat in my belly as we reached my Roadster. I started to go around to the passenger side to help him in, but thought better of it. He was injured, but not incapable.

Still trying to keep the conversation light, I joked, "Hey, I hear you're getting married soon."

He paused, giving me a funny look. "Excuse me?"

"Caleigh?"

The smile returned, if slightly smaller than before. "Right. Yeah, that came out of left field. Something to do with her father. What is it with women and their fathers? You're either trying to please them or running away from them."

I shrugged, not sure how to answer. There were women out there who had normal relationships with their dads. I just didn't know any of them.

"So you're really going through with being faux-fiancé?" I asked.

He turned toward me, as he buckled his seat belt into place—not without wincing, I noticed. One corner of his mouth lifted. "Would you have a problem with that?"

I frowned. "Of course not. Why would I?" But there was a strange tightness in my voice.

"Damn. I was kind of hoping you would."

While I could hear the teasing note in his voice, I had a feeling his words weren't all that far from the truth. I shoved my key into the ignition and changed the subject. Again.

"We have a new case. I met the wife this morning. She and her husband are a couple of swingers."

His eyes widened. "Oh, this one sounds fun. Tell me the details."

I pulled out of the parking lot. "They agreed to an open marriage, and now she fears he is being faithful. She wants proof he's sleeping around."

Danny burst into laughter. "Priceless!"

Tell me about it.

I hung a left onto Franklin Ave and headed toward the 101.

"Anyway, this one should be easy."

Danny raised an eyebrow my way. "You think?"

I scoffed. "Come on, what guy wouldn't sleep around in that situation? Most husbands do anyway."

"Not all."

I shot Danny a look. "Since when did *you* become an expert on monogamy?"

He grinned, showing off an impish dimple in his left cheek. "Touché."

"Thank you," I said.

"But, trust me, when I get married, I will become one."

"You? Married?" I shook my head. "No way. That's like the Pope suddenly putting on a yamaka."

"What, I can't settle down, start a family?"

I glanced at him. "You want kids?"

He turned his head toward the window so I couldn't see his expression. "Of course. Don't you?"

I shrugged. With the agency, Derek, the girls, and my practically non-existent love life, I hadn't thought about it in a long time. "Sure. Maybe. Some day." I cleared my throat, turning the conversion back to him. "But I've never pictured you as a dad. Didn't know you did either."

"Absolutely. I'm going to be the father that encourages little Daniella to play softball and Danny Jr. to be a nurturing caregiver. She'll help me mow the lawn, while he helps my wife bake cakes. I'll be the cool, progressive dad."

I chuckled. "How very non-gender biasing of you. Except for the part where you're mowing the lawn and your wife is baking."

He smirked.

It was sweet though. I pictured Danny on a baseball field teaching a little girl in pigtails to watch the ball as she swung. Oddly enough, the picture inspired that warm sensation to wiggle through my belly again.

I glanced at his profile.

He was staring out the window, a smile on his face. Was he imagining the same?

Maybe Danny was right. Maybe I didn't know him as well as I thought.

* * *

I bit into a large, drenched in salt, pretzel, which was cold and no longer soft, before spying through the windows of Aiden's office again. I really needed to plan for these stakeouts better and buy food that wouldn't leave me starving in thirty minutes. I was dying for a spinach salad with grilled chicken, strawberries, and almonds.

Aiden walked past his window to his desk. He sat down and scribbled on a legal pad.

I couldn't help but wonder if his long hours were just due to his workload, or if it was also a way to keep his mind off of his late wife. And me.

Miranda entered his office, in another tighter than work appropriate blouse, and handed him a file.

Or a way to get closer to his colleague.

I shook that thought off. Aiden was all business. Even if he wanted to date her, he wouldn't do it in the office. He'd call her up and ask her out on a proper date—dinner, candlelight, maybe even flowers, although I hadn't received any. He wasn't a fish tacos at a roadside joint kinda guy.

Aiden nodded and said something to her. There was no laughter or cleavage shot. I assumed they discussed a case they were working on.

Then Miranda walked out, and I expelled a breath I hadn't realized I was holding.

I continued to watch, but nothing new happened. Aiden continued working, without a glance at his watch. I wondered if he thought of me at all these days. I hadn't seen him reach for the phone or daydream in space. Nothing. Not just tonight but the other times I'd watched too. I couldn't imagine he'd forgotten about me, but that was where the evidence pointed. I'd received no messages, no heavy breathing, not even a single hang up.

I could call him. Not now, but tomorrow, and ask him to lunch. We could go to that Italian place we went to on our first date, which really wasn't a date but a way for each of us to interrogate the other. That was right after I had met him, before we realized we could trust one another. When he thought I'd murdered a judge, and I needed answers only he possessed. Of course he hadn't given me answers. He was too professional for that. But the restaurant would always be a special place.

So, yes, lunch at Franco's.

I smiled.

Then I remembered his "it's not you; it's me" speech and frowned.

No, he'd think I wasn't respecting his wishes to give him time.

Aiden shuffled papers then flipped through the file to the back and pulled out another sheet. He kneaded the back of his neck and arched his back before returning to the documents.

I could've just called him to see how he was doing. Casual, platonic, concerned. That wouldn't be pushy. One friend talking to another. Then I could gauge his emotions by his tone. If he missed me, he'd be all heady, and if he sounded business-like then I'd know I wasn't on his mind. But did I want to know the answer? What if I didn't like it?

I sighed. Why were men so exasperating?

Aiden read document after document and made a ridiculous number of notes. His hand had to be cramped.

Miranda came in two more times, but he still stayed focused on his work. That didn't mean she didn't try to deter him though.

First she used the act of dropping her pen and bending ever so slowly to retrieve it.

"Bend at the knees," I shouted to my windshield. "It's more seductive." Thrusting her ass in my face, let alone his, just made her look desperate.

Aiden looked up but quickly returned to his papers. He was either being polite or not interested. I was going with the latter.

The second time she entered his office, she brought him a cup of coffee. Instead of just handing it to him and hoping he'd join in with small talk, she raised her mug and said something, as if making a toast. This required him to put down the paperwork and play along. Smart girl. Although still desperate.

They clicked mugs and sipped their coffee. At least I assumed it was coffee. Maybe she kept a bottle of whiskey at her desk. As determined as she seemed, I wouldn't have put it pass her.

A nightcap at the office didn't seem like Aiden's thing though. He nodded and set his cup down. He pointed to the file and said something.

She gave a polite and grim smile then left his office.

"Yes! Score two…or was it more…to Prince."

There were no more interruptions from Miranda. Aiden continued working, and I may have dozed off for just a second.

I lowered the binoculars, rubbed my eyes, and knew it was time to go home.

I took one last peek through the lenses and spotted a man turning the corner of the building. He didn't come from the parking lot either, but the side street. Not an unusual event, but this part of town was only office buildings and coffee houses, and at this time, none of them were open. Then there was his gait. He had what I could only describe as a rap video swag to his step.

He walked to the front doors and peered through the glass.

My suspicious nature flared. I zoomed in on his face.

Scruffy, unshaved chin, dark eyes, hawk-like nose, and slicked down, dark hair. He wore shorts that were too baggy (thank goodness his long basketball jersey covered his underwear) and white sneakers that were so new and blinding, they called out like a beacon.

I knew him.

He'd come into The Spotted Pony, a strip joint at which I'd briefly enjoyed an undercover job while working a case a couple of years ago. It was long enough ago that I might not have recognized him, but he'd been one of the more popular customers. They'd called him Rocky. Rumor was he got the name because he always had cocaine on him. One of the dancers at the strip club had dated him while he'd supplied product to the other dancers.

I could understand him needing an attorney. He probably had a couple on speed-dial. But public defenders and the high-priced lawyers who usually worked for his type of scum didn't work in this building. So why was he interested in the DA's office at ten o'clock at night?

This was one PI about to find out.

CHAPTER THREE

As Rocky entered the building, I panicked, not sure what to grab and what to leave behind to follow him. I'd been set for surveillance, not an excursion. I snatched the keys from the ignition and slipped my phone into my bra, just in case. Unfortunately my skirt didn't have pockets. I tossed the binoculars into my purse, which was between my feet, and jumped from my seat, knocking pretzel remains onto the floor.

I locked my door and sprinted across the street; my heels click-clacked along the pavement. When I reached the double, glass doors, I hesitated. How did he get in?

The DA's offices used to be located at the criminal justice center, but recently, due to renovations and asbestos, they'd temporarily moved here. This was just a regular building, not a courthouse with metal detectors and guards, but surely their security was still tight.

I pushed one of the doors. It opened without hesitation. I never tried to access the offices during my stakeout nights. Why would I when I had a clear view from my car? So I wasn't certain if it was always unlocked or done specifically for Rocky tonight.

I ran forward and caught the tail end of him stepping onto an elevator. I hurried forward, hoping he wouldn't turn at the sound of my shoes.

As the doors whooshed shut, I lunged for the stairs. If I was fast enough, I could make it up three flights only seconds after he stepped off the elevator. I slipped off my heels and booked it. My tight pencil skirt didn't allow super-high thigh movement, so I shimmied it up until it barely covered my bottom.

By the time I reached the third floor, I was panting, mildly. I would've loved to blame it on the necessary burst of speed, but who was I kidding? I considered a workout to include lifting my binoculars while chewing overly-processed, Richard Simmons-deemed-unworthy snacks. I blamed my junk-food addiction on all those years of modeling when carbs, sweets, and oils were considered the by-product of Satan. I had years of real eating to make up for.

I staggered onto the third floor and spotted Rocky yanking open a door ahead. I took a deep, wheezing breath and stumbled forward just before it closed.

A large reception desk stood across from me. A corridor to the left and a smaller one to the right held several office doors. The walls were painted in an off-white, and a thick, burgundy carpet cushioned my soles. Several lights above the reception area were off, so the remaining few cast a soft glow along the lobby. It was bright enough to see where I was headed and to make out the surroundings well, but dim enough to hide if necessary.

Rocky walked to the other side of the reception desk and stared to his left, to something I couldn't see. He just stood there. Was he waiting for someone or lost?

As the door behind me shut with a soft thud, I watched Rocky's head turn in my direction.

Crap.

I ducked and scrambled to the front of the reception area on my hands and knees. My keys made a soft jingle, and I tucked them into my palm tighter. I held my breath and listened for the sound of footsteps headed toward me. There were none. I expelled my breath and crawled to the corner. I peered left and right, noticing another corridor, and hoped I wouldn't get lost in this maze. This floor didn't look that big from outside. If my calculations were correct, Aiden's office was down the left hall, on the right-hand side. As long as I stayed away from…

A door opened ahead, and a young man in gray slacks and a white top stepped into the hall.

Movement sounded behind me. Perhaps Rocky was hiding too. I took one crawl back, hopefully out of eyeshot, but I was still able to watch the man. He walked a few feet ahead, never glancing my way, and pushed open a door without turning a knob, probably a bathroom.

When he disappeared behind the door, I scrambled forward, still on my hands and knees, like a mouse searching for a hunk of cheese. I circled the reception area, and as I reached the side where Rocky stood, I contemplated where to hide next. I couldn't just crawl around the corner. He was only a yard in front of me. He'd have to be deaf and blind not to see the blonde woman on all fours, revealing her pink leopard panties. (Hey, it was laundry day, and they were comfortable. In hindsight, at least I hadn't worn my lacy thongs.) But I also couldn't stay in this position because my barely covered butt cheeks would be the first thing the man saw after relieving himself.

My options were to slip into the reception area and perhaps hide under the desk, or to leap for the potted tree near the back wall.

I chose the desk.

Unfortunately I didn't notice the hard, bumpy, plastic floor-covering until it dug into my knees and palms. Ouch! I jerked back, hitting my elbow into a metal drawer. Shoot.

I glanced up and around. No one peered down at me, but just in case, I grabbed a pad of paper from the desk and slowly rose, like an administrative assistant from the dead.

Rocky no longer stood in his last spot.

I hurried around the desk and peeked down the hall. It was empty. From the corner of my eye, I noticed a door closing. I ran to it, hoping to catch a glimpse inside before it shut, but by time I got there, it was only open an inch.

I contemplated pushing it further, risking someone seeing it move and finding me on the other side.

That was when I looked up and saw the name plate on the door. Steven Conrad, District Attorney.

The hamster on my mental wheel got off his fat booty and started jogging. A known drug dealer was slipping in to see the District Attorney late at night. This smacked of the sort of corruption I'd been looking for. Was this a payoff? Was the DA himself fixing cases for Rocky? Or possibly someone higher up the coke food-chain than my strip club-loving friend?

I had a hard time believing that the head of the entire Los Angeles criminal justice system was involved in something so vile. And yet...

I leaned forward, slightly bent at the waist, and pressed my ear against the crack, hoping to overhear juicy intel. But if anyone was talking, they were whispering because I couldn't hear a thing. Minutes ticked by until I heard...

"Nice panties," said an all-too familiar voice.

Chills raced down my back. I gasped and jerked upright. Oh God, please don't let that be him. Please, please, please...

I swung around and faced Aiden.

Clearly God knew I wasn't a regular church-goer.

Aiden raised his brows and gazed at my middle.

Heat ricocheted throughout my body, causing my head to ignite like a tiki torch. I wiggled my skirt back into place and said the first thing I thought of.

"Hi, there!"

I sounded like a cheerleader, painfully enthusiastic. I was sure my stupid smile hadn't helped, but I felt the corners of my mouth creep up before I could stop them.

"Hi." He said it slowly and drawn out, as he would to someone who was hard of hearing or if English wasn't their native language.

I just stared at his beautiful, yet inquisitive, eyes. I hadn't expected to actually run into him. He'd been at his desk, diligently working for the past couple of hours. Why had he stopped now?

When I didn't say anything back, he asked, "Why are you here? How'd you get in? And why was your skirt up that high?"

I opened my mouth, not sure where to start.

He raised a hand, open palm. "Actually, I don't want to know about the skirt."

I decided the full truth was the only way to go. "I got a tip from a waitress who was the girlfriend of that corrupt cop, Jack Brady."

The Brady case had only been wrapped up a week ago, but it felt like a century. Aiden had been the lead prosecutor. It not only involved him but Derek and a corrupt judge, and it was the reason Danny was shot.

Aiden's jaw tightened. At least I had his professional attention. "Go on."

"She said that someone in the DA's office might be taking bribes from someone."

He raised his brows again.

"Yeah, okay, so I know it's flimsy, but..."

"You're taking the word of a corrupt ex-cop's girlfriend?"

I blinked. "Yes. Why?"

His eyes widened. "Isn't it obvious?"

"You don't believe me."

"It's a tough sell," he hedged. But his eyes said he thought I was loony.

"Just because Brady was corrupt doesn't mean the information is wrong. Just the opposite, in fact. He'd have inside knowledge."

"And absolutely no reason to give it to you," Aiden pointed out.

"Jillian is very reliable." Granted, she'd left town shortly after the trial, just like Brady, but that didn't mean she'd lied to me or had misinformation. I was especially certain after just trailing Rocky up here.

I tried again. "Look, I've been watching the office..."

"Wait—you've been watching me?"

"Uh..." Perhaps I should have glossed over that part. "That's not important. What's important is that I just saw Rocky something-or-other walk into this building and into that office. He's a known drug dealer."

"And?"

"And he's in the DA's office right now."

"Aaaaand?" Aiden asked, drawing out the word.

I threw my hands up. "And doesn't that strike you as *odd*? I mean, why now? What are they doing in there?"

"I hope you're not insinuating that the DA is taking bribes from a drug dealer." It was a statement more than a question, once that said in no uncertain terms that I had better watch my step. Aiden was in full-on lawyer mode now, and I had a feeling anything I said could and would be used against me in the future.

"I'm saying it's *odd*," I repeated.

Aiden shook his head. "Rocky something-or-other?"

"Yes." Exactly. Was he finally believing me? "He's a known drug dealer. I met him when I worked at The Spotted Pony."

There went those brows again.

I groaned. "Not work-worked. I was undercover. It was a long time ago. It doesn't matter. What does is that Rocky dated one of the girls, and he supplied drugs to some of the other dancers and patrons."

"Did you report this Rocky something-or-other to the police?"

I rolled my eyes. "No, I didn't."

He gave me his best "ADA Aiden Prince" look, the one he usually reserved for making a witness squirm on the stand.

"Give me a break. I'm a PI not a cop. If I reported every little infraction of the law I encountered in my line of work, I'd be camping at the precinct full time."

He pinched the bridge of his nose and squeezed his eyes shut for a moment. "So instead of helping the police put away a—how did you put it?—*known drug dealer*, you were there to catch a cheating husband, and a mere criminal didn't merit blowing a simple infidelity case."

Geeze. It wasn't as if I overlooked someone being murdered.

His tone, the way he seemed to want to take every word I said and boil it down to some meaningless heap of dog doo was starting to tick me off. My hands curled. Not that I'd actually hit him, but I placed them on my hips, just the same. "That *is* my job."

"And mine is on my desk, waiting for me to get back to it."

I stood straighter, almost meeting him eye-to-eye. "So you're just going to let this *known criminal* in the next room hang out there because he doesn't merit delaying your mountain of paperwork? Wow, you really are all about justice," I said, turning the tables on him.

His eyes hardened. I'd admit I was a bit gleeful that I'd hit a nerve.

I didn't wait for him to respond. "Rocky walked in off the street, got on the elevator, walked through those doors, and into that office."

"That's not possible."

Was he calling me a liar? For a brief moment I wondered why he'd been so attractive to me before now.

"The building doors are locked after six. No one can get in without a key."

"Unless someone unlocked it on purpose so Rocky could get inside. Someone like…" I pointed to the DA's office.

He took a deep breath and exhaled it slowly. "The DA is vacationing in Hawaii with his wife for the week."

My stomach sank. Oh. That didn't sound or look good. There went my credibility.

"Fine, but I know what I saw. He entered the building, and—" I began again, in case all these hours at work were actually leeching brain cells and he needed another explanation.

But he didn't let me finish. Instead he leaned forward and pushed the door fully open.

I followed him inside as he flipped a switch, turning on an overhead. Light forced back the shadows. The office, aside from the usual furniture and a browning plant on a side table, was empty.

What the hell?

Another step in and I noticed two doors along the left wall. One was narrow, up by the back wall of windows, and shut. I assumed it was a closet. The other, however, was ajar, and it led to another office or a smaller hall. It was dark, and I couldn't make it out. Rocky must've gone through that door. He could be anywhere in the building.

And now I felt stupid.

I turned to Aiden, almost afraid to look at his expression.

But he didn't seem mad or triumphant that he'd proved me wrong. Much. The tiny lines around his eyes were soft, and the corners of his mouth were down turned a bit. If anything, he looked tired. I hated that all the reasons I'd been unable to get him out of my mind came flooding back to me.

"I don't know what to say. Obviously I was wrong about the DA, but I followed Rocky up to this floor. I don't know who he's here to see, but someone…"

Sound came from the mysterious doorway. I turned back just in time to see Miranda walk through. She held a stack of papers and smiled at Aiden, completely ignoring me. As if a stranger in the office at night was a common occurrence.

Hmm, was it?

"Do have you a minute to go over these?" she asked him.

"Of course." He glanced at me and lowered his voice. "I'm sure you know the way out."

In other words, he didn't want to catch me snooping around anymore.

I nodded. I had no intention of continuing my search. Tonight.

Aiden stood by the main office door and waited for Miranda and me to step into the hall before he pushed in a button on the knob then firmly shut the door, locking me out. He knew me too well. Then he and Miranda took a right and headed down the hall.

As I watched them discuss some legal matter, their shoulders brushing against one another with each in-sync step, I ran through what had just happened.

Rocky went into the DA's office. I was sure of that. He must've left through that side door. The same door Miranda walked through a minute later. Chances were most of the offices up here were interconnected, and walking through them to get to your destination was common. Nothing weird or suspicious.

Aiden and Miranda stopped in front of his office. As they turned and walked in, her gaze finally flickered to me. It wasn't long enough to read. She had to wonder who I was. Did she think I was Aiden's girlfriend? Probably not. His co-workers most likely knew about his wife. Maybe he even told her he wasn't dating.

Wait, how did she know Aiden and I were in the DA's office? Had she heard us from the hallway? Or had she heard us from *inside* the office, quickly slipping Rocky out the side door as someone entered?

There were too many unanswered questions, and I clearly wasn't getting those answers tonight.

I headed to the elevator.

Maybe I was seeing more than what actually existed. Yes, Rocky definitely was in here, but maybe he was simply involved with one of the secretaries.

The doors whooshed open, and I stepped onto the elevator. Nah, I didn't believe that. Brady's girlfriend was telling the truth. Someone in this office was taking bribes.

I pressed the L button.

And I'd be more than happy to learn it was Miranda Valens.

CHAPTER FOUR

———

The next morning in the office, Maya handed me my usual highly caffeinated, highly sweetened beverage, and I handed her a sticky note with Miranda's name written on it. "Can you please find me everything you can on her?"

Maya glanced at the neon pink square. "Sure. Is she a new Livingston girlfriend?"

"No. It's another case."

She frowned. I knew she hated it when I kept secrets as much as when I rifled through her uber organized drawers for a pen.

"Remember Jack Brady?" I relented.

Maya whistled. "Who could forget? Built like a brick wall and almost killed you from the backseat of your car."

Technically he was only trying to scare me. Which I refused to admit he had succeeded in doing. "His girlfriend told me there's corruption in the DA's office."

Maya shot me a knowing look then waved the sticky note, "And this woman is behind it?"

I wished. "Not sure yet. Need the intel."

"You got it." She turned to her keyboard and began typing.

"Oh, can you also find out the real name of a drug dealer called Rocky?"

Maya raised her perfectly waxed brows but this time simply nodded and jotted down a note on a pad of paper.

Caleigh stepped from her office. "Ready to go meet girlfriend number one, boss?"

"Let's go."

* * *

Half an hour later Caleigh and I were in West Hollywood at a place called Starlight. It was some night club I'd only heard of in passing. Supposedly they had live entertainment and killer mojitos. I parked in the back, and we walked around the dark blue building to ornate double doors.

Inside the overhead lights were turned up brighter than they'd ever be during business hours. A full stage lined most of the far wall, with a bar to our left and tables everywhere else. It had 'jazz club' written all over it, with teak hardwood floors and mahogany tables.

We walked down two steps and steered our way toward the bartender, who had his back to us, wiping glasses with a towel. Another man was on stage strumming a guitar, and one more wiped down the tables.

"Hi," I shouted over the beginning chords of a song.

The bartender flinched then turned. "Sorry, we're closed."

"I know. I'm looking for someone. Melanie Anderson."

The bartender visually checked us out. He may have lingered on Caleigh longer than necessary. I guessed we passed his little inspection because he pointed to the stage.

I glanced over and did a double take. A woman with curves in all the right places had stepped onto it. She walked to the standing microphone. "One, two, testing."

That was one of Stuart's girlfriends? She could not have been more opposite to his wife.

"Mind if we wait?" I asked the bartender.

He waved a hand to the tables. "Pick a seat."

Melanie opened her mouth, and a syrupy voice, thick and sultry sang the first note of a bluesy tune. She wore her brown hair in long waves—the kind that never saw frizz no matter what the weather. She had on a simple gray tunic and tight jeans with high-heeled boots, yet she still looked stunning.

I glanced to Caleigh, and we both raised our brows.

"How can the wife tolerate knowing he's been with her? I'd be jealous to death," Caleigh said.

I nodded, in complete agreement.

We chose a table up front, dead center to the stage, and sat down.

After a few minutes of watching Melanie sing, the way she swayed her hips, slow and in tune to the melody, I realized the guitar player was staring at Caleigh. A smile tugged at his mouth. He had that trendy, just-got-out-of-bed-and-I'm-still-perfect look to him. Brown hair that fell into his eyes when he played made him look more intense.

I didn't need to glance her way to know whether or not Caleigh was interested. He was her type—not too clean-cut yet not too unkempt either, somewhere between Daniel Radcliffe and Duck Dynasty.

But I looked anyway. Sure enough, she was batting her lashes and practically purring in her seat.

When the song ended, the bartender walked to the stage, pointed toward us, and whispered something to Melanie. Then he went back to prepping for tonight.

She stepped down and glided to our table. Even her walk was sultry and magnetic. "You wanted to talk to me?" she asked in a voice that could melt diamonds.

"Please have a seat," I said and pulled out a business card. "I'm Jamie Bond, and this is my associate Caleigh Presley."

Caleigh extended her arm. "Elvis Presley's distant cousin. Pleased to meet you." She said it loud. Louder than necessary for someone directly across from her. Unless, of course, she was hoping a hot guitarist overheard and was impressed.

He must've been, too, because he sat on the edge of the stage and watched her.

I refrained from eye rolling as Caleigh and Melanie shook hands.

Melanie glanced at my card. "Why does a private investigator want to speak with me?"

"We'd like to ask you some questions about a friend of yours. Stuart Livingston."

Her pale gray eyes opened wide. "Is something wrong? Is he okay?"

"He's fine. We're just, um…" I glanced at Caleigh for support, but she was too busy making goo-goo eyes with her new admirer.

"I know he's married," Melanie said and placed her left hand on the table. A large diamond ring and wedding band rested on her ring finger. "So am I."

That caught Caleigh's attention. We exchanged glances again.

"It's not as uncommon as most people think," Melanie said.

"I'm sorry. We don't mean to appear judgmental. I'm just not familiar with the lifestyle."

Melanie nodded. "Most aren't. People think we're sexual deviants or we're cheaters. That's not the case. In fact, being honest with our spouses is the key to a healthy relationship. Cheating is all about lies and betrayal. We don't want to experience the doubts, fear, and deception that come with that. We want fun and adventure, and it keeps our true relationship alive."

She made it sound so benign, yet interesting. Not that I'd ever agree to it. Maybe Derek should've tried it though.

"We were wondering if you and Stuart still saw one another." I asked.

She shook her head. "I haven't seen him in weeks."

Caleigh giggled. From the corner of my eye, I watched the guitarist blush. God only knew what Caleigh was doing beside me.

I kept my focus, as best as I could, on Melanie. "Any reason why you haven't seen him recently?"

"Every time I've called he's either busy or doesn't answer."

"Is that usual?" I asked.

"Not really. In the beginning, we couldn't get enough of each other."

As stunning as she was, I had no doubts.

"The last time you saw him, what was he like?"

She looked off, as if pulling up the memory. "Distant. He didn't pay attention to our conversation, kept looking off and wasn't involved."

"Do you know what was on his mind? Did he talk about anything troubling him?" I asked.

"He was worried about his job and his brother." She went on to explain what I'd already heard from his wife. "But I got the feeling that he was preoccupied by something else. He didn't say what though. It's a shame. I miss him. He was fantastic in bed."

I inhaled wrong and coughed. I wasn't expecting that.

Melanie glanced at her watch. "If you don't mind, I need to get going."

"Sure. Thanks for talking to us."

She smiled and walked backstage. Everyone, except the guitarist, watched her leave. He still had his attention on Caleigh.

Caleigh and I stood. I expected to walk out the front, but Caleigh went to the stage.

I should've known.

The guitar player reached out his hand.

Caleigh placed hers in his, and he brought her hand to his lips.

It looked kinda over-the-top and quirky to me, but Caleigh giggled, obviously swooned.

"I'm Curtis," he said.

She gave her usual introduction. The one that informed she was a distant cousin of Elvis. Again.

Curtis took a step closer. "Seriously? I'm super impressed."

"You should be," she said with a smirk.

They chatted and flirted for a couple more minutes before he asked the inevitable, "Can I have your number?"

She pulled a pen from her purse, but instead of handing him a business card, she grabbed a napkin from a table and wrote her digits on it. Smart move. Sometimes guys were turned off by female PIs.

As we headed outside to my car, I told her, "Now you don't need Danny. You can pretend Curtis is your fiancé."

Caleigh laughed. "Oh sure, that would go over like gangbusters. 'Hey, Curtis, let's skip the first date and just get engaged.' No thanks, I think I'll stick with marrying Danny."

I laughed along with her as we got into the car and pulled into traffic, but that unsettled sensation returned to my stomach again at the words "marrying" and "Danny" in the same breath.

And it must have registered on my face.

"You sure you're okay with me using your guy like this?" she asked.

"He's not *my* guy," I protested. Possibly a little too harshly.

Caleigh shrugged. "No, I didn't mean it like that. But, well, Danny is yours. Whether you want to admit it or not, whether you two stay friends or not. You're, like, a couple that doesn't sleep together or something."

I snorted, but part of me almost agreed with her assessment.

"Look, if this bothers you at all, I won't do it. Just say so."

Staring into her big, blue eyes, I was reminded of the woman who'd had my back many times over the years. I was touched she'd put our friendship before her lies with her father.

"I have no issues with you and Danny portraying the happy couple. Why would I? Danny and I are just friends." The words left a bad aftertaste in my mouth.

She smirked and nodded. "Uh-huh. Just as I thought." Though, luckily she dropped it until we reached the office.

My first stop as we entered the agency was Maya's desk. "Have you been able to find anything on the names I gave you?"

She set down her can of Diet Coke and nodded. "Oh, yeah. Miranda Valens is squeaky clean. She graduated Summa Cum Laude from Harvard with a degree in political science and then went on to law school. She's never been married, no kids, and has worked at the DA's office for six years."

Maya gave me a pointed look. "They snapped her up right after graduating third in her class."

With those kinds of achievements, she could've worked at a number of high profile law firms, yet she chose to work for the state, which was famous for lousy hours and even lousier pay. Was she just a Good Samaritan who believed in justice, like Aiden? If so, they were perfect for each other.

Maya tapped her notepad. "She's rich too."

I rolled my eyes. Of course she was. "Is her family wealthy?"

"Nope. Her dad works at a dry cleaner's in Long Beach, and her mother is a maid at a Best Western in Anaheim. No, Miranda's money is her own."

My radar flared. I almost gleefully rubbed my hands together and cackled at the prospect of taking her down. "How rich is she?"

Maya trailed her finger down the page. "We aren't talking Donald Trump, but she just bought a new house in Pasadena and sends money to her mother each week."

My elation crumbled. That wasn't overly suspicious. Maybe she'd been saving up for the past six years. Maybe she got a rock-bottom interest rate, or one of those low down payment loans. "Any connection between her and Rocky? What's his real name?"

Maya shook her head. "Rocco Diaz, and no, his name didn't come up."

Damn. I seriously wanted to connect dots between those two.

"By the way, a woman named Elaine called for you." Maya handed me a pink slip of paper with Elaine's name and number on it. I shoved it into my purse, hoping I could put off Derek's lie as long as possible. That was one conversation I was not looking forward to.

"Okay, well let's run down the deets for Rocco Diaz."

Maya flew into action, pulling up windows and typing along. "He has a girlfriend, Vanessa Estevez, and a couple of kids. They rent an apartment in Inglewood, a couple of blocks east of La Brea."

Not exactly the nicest area. I didn't expect him to spill his guts to a couple of strangers, or to anyone for that matter. But maybe I could get some info from the girlfriend.

Maya jotted down the address and handed it to me.

I was about to turn to see if Sam or Caleigh were free, when the front door opened.

A tall man wearing a white suit and a white Stetson sauntered toward me. He removed his hat upon seeing us and smiled widely. "Excuse me, but I'm looking for Miss Caleigh Presley. Might I find her here?"

His accent was thick and southern. His light blue eyes twinkled and, coupled with a thin nose that turned up ever so slightly at the end and a narrow chin, he was the spittin' image of his daughter. Or the other way around.

Then it hit me. He was a week early. Oh crap.

I nodded to Maya, who scrambled off, and extended my hand. "Mr. Presley? I'm Jamie Bond. Caleigh works for me."

He cocked a brow and gave me the body check, but not in a threatening way. "Well, you aren't a man."

I chuckled loudly, but not in a happy way. "No, sir, I'm not."

He rubbed his chin. "Oh gosh, I didn't mean to sound insulting, but when my baby girl said she worked for a private investigator, I assumed she meant a man."

Obviously Caleigh didn't share much of her life with dear ol' Dad.

"Daddy?" Caleigh sounded as struck with fear as she looked—eyes bulged, mouth drooped.

Mr. Presley held his arms wide open. "Come to Daddy, darlin'."

Caleigh ran into her father's arms and laid her cheek on his shoulder. For a moment, she looked happy and at peace. Then it quickly changed, and the panic returned to her face with lines crinkling between her brows.

Maya and Sam joined my side. Sam and I exchanged looks but didn't say a word. What was the likelihood Daddy forgot his darlin' was fake-engaged?

"You're early," Caleigh said.

"I wanted to surprise you."

She turned to us with a forced smile.

"Surprise," Maya, Sam, and I said in unison.

Her frown deepened. I didn't think she found us amusing.

"I would've met you at your apartment, but I wasn't sure what time you'd be off work," he added.

"Notforawhile." Her words tumbled out so fast, they slurred into one.

"I hope this isn't a bad time." He looked around the empty reception area.

She took a deep breath and exhaled slowly. "No, Daddy. I just wasn't prepared yet. I planned to have my place ready and to take off a couple of days from work to show you around. But I can't do that on such short notice."

She glared at me for help.

Sam nudged me with her elbow.

I found my voice. "Yes, I'm sorry. We're swamped with clients, and Caleigh has a huge case-load. I couldn't possibly do without her just now."

Mr. Presley scratched his head. "Well, that's alright, princess. I'm a grown man. I don't need to be entertained. I will see you when you're done working. Although I'd love to see your office and hear more about your work while I'm here."

Caleigh smiled. "Of course, Daddy. I'd love to show you." She held out a hand. "My office is this way."

They took a few steps, and he stopped. "I know this is short notice, but I do hope you three beautiful young ladies will allow an old man to take you to dinner tonight?"

Caleigh laid a hand on his arm and giggled. "You're not old, Daddy."

That so wasn't the point.

Before I could open my mouth to protest, Maya said, "I'm free tonight."

Mr. Presley looked to me, but Sam replied, "I can find a babysitter."

Great. Now I had no choice.

It wasn't that I didn't want to get to know Caleigh's father. I just wasn't ready for the lying and pretending portion of the evening. Of course, the plus side was another free meal, and I had a feeling Daddy would pick someplace more elegant than a roadside taco joint.

"This is very generous of you," I said. "I'd be happy to join you." My first lie of the night, and I had a strong feeling it wouldn't be the last.

"Good." He turned back to his daughter. "When we're done here, you can give me your key, and I'll settle in at your place. Then at dinner you can introduce me to my future son-in-law."

Oh, boy.

CHAPTER FIVE

———

It didn't take Caleigh long to show her dad around and dazzle him with a couple of old cases we'd worked. I noticed how she didn't mention any that were too scandalous, like the actress posing as a wife, the nudist husband, the panty thief, our current swingers, or even the gay couple. She asked for an hour off to drive her father to her place, to help settle him in, and to make sure she hadn't left anything embarrassing out in the open—like her vibrator. I was a very accommodating boss.

On their way out Mr. Presley waved and shouted, "Don't forget tonight."

Like I could if I wanted to.

As they walked out, I took Sam aside and explained what was happening over at the DA offices.

"How can I help?" she asked.

I grabbed my purse from my bottom desk drawer. "Go with me to check out this Vanessa Estevez and find out what we can about Rocco."

"Sure thing."

We pulled up in front of Vanessa and Rocco's home, a two-story former motel turned apartment building that clearly needed to be condemned. Boarded up front windows in half the units, loose shingles, and a broken concrete walkway. A line of beat-up, rusted cars bookended a late model SUV at the curb. And on a pathetic strip of dried grass than ran between the buildings sat a popped beach ball and an overturn tricycle.

At the corner, a small circle of guys hung out, they're eyes shifty enough that even to the casual observer they were obviously up to something. Two cars had slowed down in the past ten minutes we'd been parked here. One of the guys would step to the passenger window, lean in, and he and the driver would make exchanges. It was all done so openly. They obviously weren't afraid of the cops, or more likely, the police didn't drive by this part of town too frequently. The beat cops weren't stupid.

"What's the plan, boss?" Sam asked.

The address Maya had given me listed a unit 104 on the ground floor as belonging to Rocco. The curtains were drawn, and there was no sign of life inside. I dialed the office. "Not sure yet."

"Bond Agency, how may I help you?" said Maya.

"It's me. Can you run a plate, please?" I rattled off the numbers and letters of the SUV and waited for her to do her magic. Even if Rocco were a low level dealer, there's no way that swaggering guy would be caught dead in any of the other junk-yard rejects at the curb.

One of the men at the corner stared in our direction. He'd been watching us since just after we'd arrived. Now he pointed to us. It was time for us to make a move. The last thing we needed was them coming this way and causing a scene. We'd never get to speak to Vanessa then.

I looked to Sam and said, "How do you think we should play this?"

"She has kids, so…"

"Social workers." It was the easiest way. Into the phone, I said," Got anything yet, Maya?"

I heard her fingers clicking on the keyboard. "Yes. It belongs to Rocco Diaz."

Damn. If he was home, we couldn't talk to…

"But he has two cars registered to him, and the other is a Ford Mustang."

What was the likelihood that he let his girlfriend drive the sports car with the tiny backseat not big enough for two car seats?

"Thanks, Maya," I said and hung up. "I think that's her car."

"Sure hope so," Sam said.

I turned to the rearview mirror and pulled my hair back into a makeshift bun. I grabbed my jacket from the back seat and shrugged it on, all while keeping my eye on the guys. So far, they remained on the corner, but more were watching us now.

Sam wiggled her skirt low enough so it almost met her knees. Thankfully her top was long enough to meet the top of the skirt and not show off her navel. Last I knew, social workers didn't go to work with skin showing.

We stepped out of the car, and I opened the trunk for more supplies. I kept a small box with random items for just these occasions. I pulled out an empty manila envelope, an old auto body receipt from my last tune-up, and a couple of pages from last year's edition of Vogue. The black leather handbag in them was to-die-for.

I stuffed the papers into the folder, grabbed a clipboard, then dug to the bottom of the box for a pen. I slammed the trunk down, and we went across the street. The walkway was worse close up. My heels got stuck twice in the cracks, and once I twisted my ankle with such a jerk that I almost went down.

Safely at the door to 104, Sam knocked while I peered into the windows. The curtains might have been drawn, but they were threadbare. I spotted two young kids seated on a ratty sofa. They were watching SpongeBob on a big, flat screen TV. Part of the wallpaper was torn off the wall above it, and a back window looked like it hadn't been washed in a year, but on the coffee table sat a Juicy handbag and an iPad.

The front door opened, and I jerked back. The woman was probably in her mid-twenties. She wore red skinny jeans, a pink ruffled blouse with tiny white flowers, and gold sandals. Maybe she was colorblind?

"Can I help you?"

I flashed my fake badge. The generic one that didn't have a specific seal or insignia. Danny had made it on his computer, like a high-schooler hoping to buy alcohol. "Hi, we're from Child Protective Services, and we'd like to speak with Vanessa Estevez. Is that you?"

Her eyes widened for a second; then a twitch began at the corner of her mouth. "What do you want? My kids are well fed and cared for."

"May we come in, please?" I asked, not wanting to have this conversation outside, just in case the corner guys decided to investigate the two strangers.

Vanessa hesitated, looking to each of us and then inside her home. "We're about to leave."

"Just for a minute," I said with a reassuring smile, or so I thought.

But she stood firm and didn't allow us access.

"We're not from INS or the IRS," Sam said, jumping into the conversation.

I took her lead. "That's right."

I wasn't sure if Vanessa was legal or not. Maya hadn't mentioned anything. But she relaxed her shoulders and took a step back. "Okay."

I smiled and stepped over the threshold. Sam followed on my heels.

As I suspected from outside, the interior needed new wallpaper, new flooring, and even the furniture was unlivable. The kids glanced up at us but then went straight back to watching their cartoons. A boy and a girl, they wore new-looking footie pajamas—one was a dinosaur and the other a princess. The girl clutched a baby doll, and I thought of Danny and his progressive teachings. They didn't exist in this home.

Vanessa led us into the small kitchenette and pointed to the lopsided, round table. "Please sit."

Sam and I took a seat. I leaned on the table, and it titled toward me. I removed my arms and sat back, praying the spindly chair legs wouldn't crush beneath my weight.

"Coffee? It only does one cup at a time, but I can make it twice," Vanessa asked, pointing to a shiny, new Keurig Brewer. It sat beside an old stove with grease buildup on the back wall. Everything else was clean though—the counters, the table, even the floor. It was worn and spotted from wear and tear, but it was obvious Vanessa took pride in what they had.

I shook my head. "No thank you. We're here about…" I looked down to the folder, flipped it open, and pretended to read from documents. "Um, Rocco Diaz. There's no employment listed, and we're inquiring about his income, co-workers…"

"He's a good man. He plays with the kids and bathes them." She twisted her hands together and stared at her children. "They love him."

"I'm sure they do," I said in between her frantic pleas to inform us he was a great father. Her nervousness was making me jumpy.

"Just the other day, he took them to the park. Not the one down the street because it's not clean and the swings are broken, but one someplace else. Where the rich people live. They had so much fun. The kids came back exhausted and took a long nap. They're good kids."

I opened my mouth to interrupt, but she kept on talking.

"I know this place isn't that nice, but I keep it clean, and we buy the kids what they need. We pay our bills on time. Never late. The kids start school in one and two years. I stay home with them, and I never leave them alone. Never." Her voice cracked. "If Rocco and I want to go out and be sexy, we take them to my mother's in Riverside. No babysitters. Ever.

Sam looked away again. She stared into the living room. As a single mom, she didn't have that luxury. Julio spent most of his time at school or with sitters. Our job demanded flexibility. Did Sam feel bad about that? She never talked about it. The only conversations we had about Julio were on how great he was doing in school, or how he had a crush on a girl named Cherry. And how in high school, that name would haunt her. She'd be forever asked if she'd been popped yet.

"My son can write his own name, and my daughter knows how to count to one hundred. Aye, Papi, show these nice ladies how you write your name," she called out to the little boy.

He looked up, dazed for a second. I doubted he'd been following our conversation.

"No," I said loud enough for him to hear. "That's fine."

He turned his eyes back to the television. That must've been one enthralling sponge.

"We don't smoke. Well, I don't. Rocco used to, but he gave it up over the summer. He's gone two months without a cigarette. And we don't drink, except on special occasions. Like we had a bottle of champagne on New Year's Eve. I buy lots of milk and chicken for the kids, to keep their bones healthy. I try to buy fruits but sometimes they're expensive, or the stores in this area don't have them fresh. They're rotten."

Oh dear God, did this woman ever shut up? I wasn't trying to be mean. Granted, I just hinted that we could take her kids away, but if she'd stop talking long enough to listen to what we wanted, we'd already be gone.

"Ms. Estevez, we're here to talk about Mr. Diaz's job," I shouted over her.

"He works hard, and he buys us nice clothes. I show you?" She pointed down the hall.

The last thing I wanted was a fashion show, especially considering what she currently wore. I shook my head. "There's no need for that. We just want to make sure he has the means to support your children, otherwise…"

I let the threat hang and immediately felt like a jerk for doing it. She obviously felt scared or threatened already, or she wouldn't have been rambling so much.

Sam glanced at me then turned to Vanessa. "We don't want to cause you any problems. It's obvious that the kids are well dressed and safe."

Spying the chipped paint on the ceilings, I felt Sam pulled that last word out of her butt, but didn't comment.

"We only want to know where Mr. Diaz works, so we can make sure. This visit is just a simple check."

Sam totally watered down my threat, my edge, but when Vanessa asked, "Oh, that's all?" it didn't seem to matter.

"That's all." Sam reassured her with a smile.

Vanessa expelled a breath. "Okay. He works at the car shop on Century. Ventura's."

"Thank you," I said.

"Is that all?"

I nodded. "Yes."

We stood, thanked her again, and smiled at the children on our way out. Vanessa clicked the door shut behind us.

As we hurried back to my car, I glanced at the guys at the corner. A new car had arrived, and one of the men was leaning in the driver's window. Once settled in the driver's seat, I pulled out my phone and called the office.

"Bond Agency." Maya must've been busy because her greetings are usually more extravagant.

"Maya, get me the deets for a Ventura's on West Century." In this part of town, I doubted they had mechanics who could afford to keep Vanessa and her kids in Juicy and Apple products. Obviously Rocco's dealing had something to do with their assets, so was the car shop on the up-and-up or a front for drugs?

"Okay, boss, hold on."

I covered the mouthpiece with my hand and asked Sam. "You okay?"

She nodded. "Would you mind if I took an hour off, too? I'd like to pick up Julio from school and spend a little time with him before the sitter arrives."

Sam hired an older woman to watch Julio after school, but Rosa also helped her own daughter with her grandson. This meant Julio was home alone for an hour before Rosa got to Sam's house. He was a smart kid. Knew to never use the stove unless supervised, to not answer the door, and what to do in an emergency. Sam didn't usually worry about him.

I couldn't help but wonder how much Vanessa's ramblings had affected Sam, caused her to second-guess her own mothering. "No problem, I'll drop you at your car." I paused. "You sure you're okay?"

She shrugged, but I could tell there was more she was keeping back. I didn't say anything, just waited for her to open up. Hopefully it would be before Maya got back on the line to give me the address.

Finally she said, "Telling a mother you're from social services is a scary thing. You hear stories about how CPS takes kids away for small things, and you feel like you have little control."

"But if you love your kids and raise them well, there's no reason for CPS in your life. Plus, you're a great mother." She had no reason to compare herself to Vanessa. Sam may have been a single parent, but she was able to give Julio more than Rocco's kids had, and I wasn't thinking of fancy gadgets.

She gave a half-smile. "I know I am, but I'm not always around. I'm pretty sure Vanessa thinks she's a great mother too.

And she may be, but one look at this block and we assumed the worse."

She was right.

"Okay, boss, you ready?" Maya's voice filled my ear.

I took down the address she rattled off.

I dropped Sam off and drove to the shop, but half an hour later I still couldn't get Sam's words out of my head. I thought of Sam with Julio and what a great kid he was: smart, funny. That made me think of Danny again and his new revelation about kids of his own someday. Who knew, maybe he would be a good dad. I wondered...would I be a good mom? My own mother had passed away, leaving Derek to raise me. Which had hardly provided a stellar example of parenting. I'd fallen asleep in the back seat of his car on late night stakeouts more often than I had in brand new footie pajamas in my own bed. For that matter, did I want kids? Let's face it, my life was hardly conducive to leading a Girl Scout troop or heading the PTA bake sale. Then again, if a guy like Danny could surprise me, maybe I could surprise myself...

A horn honked, pulling me from my thoughts. I'd swerved into the next lane. Jerking back, I smiled apologetically at the car beside me.

The driver of a black Benz flipped me the bird.

Stay aware, Jamie. No sense in getting into a wreck because of some crazy daydream.

CHAPTER SIX

———

If I'd been paying more attention when Maya gave me the address, I would've been prepared for the spidery feeling that crawled along my skin as I pulled up to Ventura's. It looked like a regular body shop: parked cars, oil cans, spare tires, greasy rags. But a scary air of silence mingled with three thugs positioned around a white Camaro. They all glanced up when I pulled in.

I should've driven away, but that wasn't my style. Besides, how else would I get answers?

Then two beefy guys with tattooed sleeves for arms walked over. I swallowed hard when I realized one of the tats was a snake eating a mouse. Yuck!

I switched off the car, grabbed my phone (in case I needed to dial 911), and stepped out. "Hi," I said to Snake Man.

His gaze wandered from my toes to the top of my head and rested on my chest for several seconds before finally finding my eyes. His face contorted into a snarl. "Are you lost?"

His tone was so full of menace that it took me a moment to swallow and respond. "I've been hearing a strange sound and saw your shop. I'm hoping you have time to take a look."

He walked around the car, examining the exterior, but also keeping his gaze on me. I couldn't figure out if he was gauging my reaction or wanting to steal my hubcaps.

His friends walked over and stood at my hood. One watched Snake Man while the other stared me down—hard and full of anger. Obviously none of them knew how not to scare away new business. Assuming they actually worked on cars here, and the Camaro and filthy rags weren't just for show.

I swallowed twice and tried to keep my composure, but a thin layer of fear pressed my blouse to my back.

Snake Man came up behind me, raising the hairs on the back of my neck. I leaned toward my car to get away from his odor of tobacco and stale coffee. "Keys," he said under his breath.

I pointed to the ignition, where they still hung. Then I quickly backed away, glad to have him out of my personal space. The back of my legs hit the edge of a folding chair, and I sat in it to calm my nerves.

Snake Man leaned into my window and popped the hood.

His buddies lifted it, and soon the three were fiddling around inside.

I flipped through my phone and found Angry Birds and began playing, hoping they'd hear the music.

One did and glanced up.

I smiled and said, "I'm addicted to this stupid game."

As far as I could tell, Rocco wasn't here. And there was no way these three were going to volunteer any information, especially not about a friend or a corrupt DA. My only option was to at least find out who these guys were. Maybe they were connected to more than this shop. And hopefully that connection would lead to the DA's office.

"What kind of sound do you hear?" asked Snake Man.

I touched the camera app and got them all into focus. "Um, it kinda goes like, click-click-click-sshh." Hopefully my ridiculous rendition of fake car problems derailed them from noticing that the game music no longer played.

As they continued looking for a problem, I switched off my flash, muted the volume, and snapped several photos. It wasn't natural to play a game up near your eyes, so I had to yawn, sneeze, and stretch to get decent shots. I must've looked like a loon.

Finally one of the guys walked to my window and leaned in. The car roared to life. They listened for half a second then turned to me.

I jumped to my feet. The look in all three sets of eyes told me they knew there was nothing wrong with the car. And they knew I was full of shit.

Snake Man walked toward me.

Adrenaline shot through my legs, and I sprinted to my door. It didn't matter that one of the guys still blocked it. I'd push past him or climb through the passenger window if I had to. That may not have been the best or most logical plan, but I knew I needed to get out of here now.

They, of course, had other plans.

Snake Man stood directly in my path. The other two flanked my sides.

"Thank you for looking. Hopefully the sound won't start again. Do I owe you anything?" If they said yes, I'd have to get into my car to get my purse. That would be a plus.

But I was naive to think it would be that simple.

"There's nothing wrong with your car. Why are you really here?" Snake Man hissed.

"I don't know what you're talking about." I attempted to turn away and walk around his thugs, when one grabbed my bicep and yanked me back.

"Hey, get off me," I shouted and slapped him on the shoulder. Like that would've done any good, other than pissing him off more.

But his eyes didn't darken and his jaw didn't clench. In fact, he smiled and laughed, like he enjoyed the pain.

Creepy.

"What do you say we teach the pretty lady a lesson for wasting our time," he said to Snake Man.

I definitely didn't like the sound of that. Why hadn't I held onto my purse when I got out of the car? Then these assholes would be looking down the barrel of my Glock. Needless to say, I felt incredibly vulnerable.

The guy behind me caressed my hair, and I officially freaked. I tried to wiggle out of the first guy's grasp, but it did no good. His grip was too strong. Then I tried stomping on sneaker-clad feet with my heels, but it became a game of Whac-A-Mole, and these guys were winning.

They all laughed and seemed to be egged on by my desperate antics.

I doubted anyone around would come to my aid, but just in case, I screamed.

"Do you really think someone in these parts would save a skinny, white girl?" asked Snake Man with laughter.

His friends joined in. Passersby would've thought this was a regular hootenanny, except I wasn't hooting or nannying, and there wasn't anyone passing.

I jerked free and finally they let go. Unfortunately I hadn't been expecting it and lurched forward. I fell onto the cracked cement, on my hands and knees, and managed to slide forward. My arms buckled beneath me, and my face grazed the ground. My cheek burned, but I didn't have time to care.

I jumped to my feet and scrambled to my car, terrified one of them would grab me again. But no one reached for me. When I got into my seat, rolled up the windows, and locked all doors, I looked up. They were standing in a row, staring at me, arms folded across their chests.

My tires screeched as I backed out of the shop and flew over a speed bump.

Heart racing, my pulse pounded, and the burning sensation on my face intensified. Then my knees started to burn, but I wouldn't slow down until I was far away.

My phone sitting in my lap rang, and I yelped. I snatched it up and didn't glance at the caller ID. "Yeah?"

"Jamie?" It was Danny.

I took a deep breath and tried to sound normal. "Hi."

"What's wrong?"

Obviously my acting sucked. Good thing I never tried to get into that profession.

"Nothing. What's up?" I bit my lip to steady my voice.

"Um, are you still picking me up?"

I glanced at the clock. It said three-ten. Shoot. I was late. "Sorry. I got behind."

"If you're too busy, I can try to find someone else." His tone was tight, like he knew something was wrong.

"No, I'm on my way." I couldn't leave Danny stranded, even if the only thing I wanted right now was a long, hot, luxuriant bubble bath.

"Okay. See you soon."

"Yep." I clicked off the call and headed back to the 101.

* * *

When I pulled up to front of the entrance, Danny was waiting outside. He opened the passenger door as I checked out my legs. Both knees were scraped and bloody. Not too bad, but they hurt like hell, and it looked like I was ten and had fallen off my bike. A quick glance in the rearview mirror showed that my chin was scraped too, just as I suspected. I didn't have time to cover it up. Danny would definitely notice.

He settled into his seat and managed to fasten his seatbelt with only half a wince. Improvement. Then he turned to me with a smile.

Which immediately faded.

"What the hell happened to you?"

I pulled out of the parking lot and headed toward his apartment. "What do you mean?" I didn't think playing dumb would work, but it was worth a shot.

"Your face. Were you in a fight with a cheese grater?"

Geeze, I didn't think I looked that bad. "No, I just fell."

"On your face?"

"Yeah." I kept my focus on driving, pretending the traffic was far more interesting than this conversation.

He took a deep breath and said, "Okay, start at the beginning."

I could've lied. I did it all the time with clients and even Derek. But lying to Danny was different. He was my best friend, my buddy, my…who the hell knew.

"I went by this body shop, looking for some information on one of its employees."

"And you tripped over a spare tire?"

"Something like that." He didn't need all the grisly details.

"Which shop?"

"Um, Ventura's. It's over on…"

"Century. Yeah, I've heard of it. There's nothing but criminals and drugs there."

I glanced at him. How did he know that?

"How could you go there on your own? At the very least, why didn't you bring Sam or Caleigh?"

"Sam had to pick up Julio from school, and Caleigh is at her apartment with her father planning your wedding."

That shut him up for a moment. But just a moment. "I thought he was coming next week. Why is he early?"

I shrugged, glad the conversation switched gears. "He wants to interrogate his future son-in-law?"

"Look, you should've waited to go to Ventura's until after you'd picked me up."

Damn, this man had a one-track mind. While the idea that he wanted to protect me was kind of endearing, I hated his belief that I needed protection.

"I'm a big girl. I know how to handle myself. I don't need hand holding."

"Your face says otherwise."

He reached into his duffel bag, pulled something out, then plopped it into my purse.

Some jerkwad ahead of me swerved into the next lane and then back into mine, so I couldn't take my eyes off the road to have a look.

"What the hell is that?" I asked, annoyed at both the driver ahead of me and the passenger beside me.

"A bug."

To hell with the road, my eyes whipped to Danny. "You just put a bug in my purse?!"

"It's so I can keep tabs on you." He held up a walkie-talkie like thing that I knew was the listening end to the intrusive bug he'd just planted on me.

"Seriously? You're baby-monitoring me now?"

"Obviously you need it."

Obviously?

I made a sharp left turn, nearly flinging him into my lap. He groaned as the seatbelt dug into his shoulder. A wee bit of guilt hit me. But just a *wee* bit.

"I know you think you're being helpful, but really, you're not."

Why was it that all men felt they knew best? Or was it just the men in my life?

"This isn't about me. It's about you throwing yourself into dangerous situations. And this isn't the first time." He clenched his jaw, as if he expected to win this argument.

I pulled up to his apartment building and slammed on the brakes. "First off, I'm a licensed PI. Danger comes with the job. Secondly, planting a bug on me isn't going to change that. And third…" I pushed the button on his seatbelt. It whipped across him and snapped into place with a crack. Then I leaned across his lap and pushed open the door. "Get out of my car."

"That's it? You're just throwing me out without discussing this?"

"Oh, but I thought you knew best for me. Obviously there's nothing to discuss, right? What could I possibly have to say about my own life?"

"You're behaving childishly." His calm tone only infuriated me more.

"Out."

As he reached for his duffle, I snatched the walkie-talkie from his grip.

"Hey," he said and reached for it.

I tossed it between my seat and door. "Nope. Now out. I've got dangerous errands to run."

For some reason he didn't fight me. I expected another round. But he stepped out onto the curb and shut my door.

And I sped off.

CHAPTER SEVEN

———

By time I reached the office I was no longer irritated, but I still needed that bubble bath. There was something about driving with the top down, the wind in my hair that made my blood pressure drop and left me more capable of a conversation without hissing. My knees ached, and I felt like a stiff, old lady, but at least I was in slightly better spirits. My injuries had to wait a little longer though. Business came first.

I pushed the front door open and was greeted by the pungent smell of burnt popcorn. Maya was walking to her desk, a bag of the charred, microwaved stuff in hand. She stopped short and gasped. "What happened to your face?"

I waved away her words as if it wasn't a big deal. "I just fell."

"Where? On a cheese grater?"

Seriously? If she insisted or even suggested I wear a wire next time, those *better spirits* would disintegrate, and I was going to lose it.

Instead she just eyed me suspiciously, and when I didn't answer her or elaborate, she continued around the desk. She knew that if I wanted to share I would. And if I didn't, it was healthy to her employed status not to pry.

I focused on her. The crusts of a sandwich and a can of Diet Coke sat beside her monitor.

"You work too much if you're eating at your desk. Why not get out of here and have lunch with Brandon? The two of you are still seeing each other, right?"

Her face flushed, so I took that as a yes.

Brandon Duke was Maya's ex-fiancé, who then became a client, and now was back where he belonged, by Maya's side, the good guy wearing the white hat. She didn't talk about them as a couple much, but since he'd come back into her life, she smiled more and was peppier in the morning. If that was possible.

To keep her from feeling she needed to answer *my* prying, I changed the subject. "Has Caleigh returned?"

"She's in her office."

"Great." I pulled up the photos I took of Snake Man and his buddies on my phone and set it on Maya's desk. "There are five shots that I took at Ventura's. Three guys. Can you find out who they are?"

Maya pulled my SD card out of my phone and pushed it into the computer slot. She clicked a few buttons, copying them over, then ejected the card. "What else do you need?"

"I want to know what court cases they've been involved in."

She pushed the card back into my phone and handed it over. "Sure thing."

Always so efficient. I never had to worry.

I walked to Caleigh's door and knocked.

"Come in." But the voice wasn't hers.

I stepped inside and saw both of my associates. While Caleigh sat behind her desk, Sam was seated in one of the chairs facing her.

They both shouted, "What happened to your face?"

I needed to remember to keep an extra tube of concealer in my purse. I took the third chair and explained Ventura's.

Lines formed between Sam's brows. "I'm so sorry I left you. If I would have stayed, I could've had your back."

"No, this isn't your fault. I should have waited for backup." Although I'd never admit that to Danny.

I looked to Caleigh. "So how'd it go with your father?"

She rolled her eyes. "That man is so exasperating."

"He seems sweet," Sam said.

Caleigh slapped her hand on her desk. "Let me tell you. He complained that I don't have an automatic ice maker, HBO, or a fireplace. It's L.A. in September, and I have an active social life. I don't need those things. Although an ice maker would be nice."

I smirked.

"I'm glad he's here. I've missed him, but when he gets here I remember why I wanted to leave home to begin with." She huffed.

"And tonight? Are things settled for dinner?" Sam asked.

"Not really. Danny doesn't want to go out tonight, so I'm gonna have to make something up about why he's not joining us."

I wondered if our little spat had anything to do with his uncooperative mood. I didn't want to make things more difficult for Caleigh, but I was relieved I wouldn't have to make small talk with him tonight.

"We're meeting at seven at Ma Belle's on Glenoaks."

I arched my brows very high. "I've never been there." I'd also never heard of it.

"Daddy wants to go to a place that serves southern food. He's been on the Internet all day searching for the perfect restaurant. He's afraid…" She used her fingers to make air quotes. "*Typical* L.A. fare is full of seaweed and soy."

Well there went my chances for a posh dining experience. Not to say southern food couldn't be posh, but anything located north of the 134 seriously depleted the chances. I glanced at my phone. It was almost four. "Maya called ahead. Livingston's second girlfriend will be at work around five-thirty. We're still on for that?" I asked Caleigh.

She nodded. "Yes."

Great. I had enough time to run home and take that bath. I stood. "Okay, I'll be back to pick you up." To Sam I said, "Go home. Spend a few hours with your son before meeting us at the restaurant."

She smiled, excitement dancing in her eyes. "You sure?"

"Absolutely." I walked to the door, waving over my shoulder.

* * *

I drove home and started peeling off my clothes right as I kicked my front door shut. My blouse by the coffee table, skirt at the bedroom door, and undergarments on the bathroom rug. I'd collect them later. As the tub filled, I poured a small glass of wine and took it back to the bathroom.

I eased myself into the hot, bubbling water, and sighed so loud I was surprised the bubbles hadn't burst. The scrapes on my knees burned for a second, but then the pain eased away. I sipped the wine, lay back, shut my eyes, and relaxed. I had to keep aware of the time. But all I needed was just a moment of nothing. No talking, no bad guys, no clients...

Then Danny popped into my mind. Of course.

His tousled hair, green eyes, boyish grin, and that stupid bug.

I opened my eyes. I hadn't wanted to get pissed again. He meant well. I guessed. In some caveman kinda way. Then I imagined Danny dressed in fig leaves, or was that pre-caveman wear? I giggled despite my irritation.

* * *

The West-side Roller Rink was located just east of Alvarado, bordering Filipinotown. I parked my car beside a pumpkin orange Honda Civic, careful to leave plenty of space between us. Caleigh and I walked to the front door in silence. We hadn't said much on the way over either. The bath and few sips of wine had relaxed me. My knees were sore, especially when bending them, but my face no longer hurt. I applied a pound of concealer and foundation and hoped it didn't cake off before the night was over.

I had dressed in a pair of leopard print pumps and a simple black dress that I could easily toss a blazer over (like now) or dress up with a simple strand of pearls (for dinner), while Caleigh wore a skin-tight, red mini dress with cap sleeves. She looked stunning, as usual. Of course, in her impress-Big-Daddy outfit, she looked a bit overdressed for a roller rink.

As soon as I entered, I squinted. The lobby was dim, and it took a minute for my eyes to adjust. Rock music blasted from speakers, and the closer we got to the rink itself, shouts and cheers mixed in with it. Three women raced around the rink, grunting. They all wore electric blue helmets and tops, with black, knee-length leggings, knee, elbow, and wrist pads, and, of course, roller skates.

"Roller derby?" Caleigh shouted into my ear.

I'd been so preoccupied this week, when Maya had given me the address of the roller rink, I hadn't questioned why. I assumed the girlfriend worked for the rink, not that she was on a team.

"Can I help you?" asked a voice to our left.

I turned to find a woman in the same color gear as those skating. "We're looking for Nikki Barnes," I told her.

The woman called over her shoulder. "Yo, Nikki. A couple of chicks to see ya."

Classy.

Before rolling off, she winked at me. "Love the shoes."

Caleigh's phone beeped. She withdrew it from her purse and smiled at the display.

I didn't ask.

"I'm Nikki." I looked over and once again was greeted by a stunning woman. She had pitch black hair pulled back into a low ponytail with full bangs. Deep set, light brown eyes and a smooth olive complexion. Her arms and legs, however, were almost covered in blue and yellow bruises. She held her helmet which had two, large, white stars on each side.

I felt right at home with the bruising.

"Hi, I'm Jamie and this is Caleigh." I didn't bother with the full introductions, didn't think we needed them, and didn't want to hear Caleigh's Elvis rendition. "We're here about Stuart Livingston."

"Is he alright?" Panic rose in her voice.

He really was loved. Not sure why that surprised me. But I guess I had a hard time reconciling the idea of a man who was sleeping his way through the entire San Fernando Valley as the big teddy bear type.

"Can you tell us about the last time you saw him?"

"Um, let me see. We went to dinner and then back to my place." She glanced over her shoulder to her teammates.

"How did he seem?" I asked.

"Uptight about his job, and he was quiet, but that's kinda normal. He's more of a doer than a talker, if you know what I mean." She winked.

Oh, I understood.

"When did you last see him?"

"It hasn't been for a few weeks. I miss him too. He was great in bed."

"Nikki, come on," shouted one of the other girls.

"I gotta go. Are we done?" She pushed her helmet onto her head.

"Sure. Thanks," I said.

"No problem." Nikki turned and rolled toward her team.

Caleigh and I watched them for a little bit, though I had a feeling I'd gotten all I was going to out of Nikki. Her story was exactly like the first girlfriend's had been. Great in bed, quiet guy, distracted the last time she'd seen him. I was beginning to get the feeling that our very easy case might very well end in the only woman in the world unhappy to hear her husband isn't cheating.

I watched the roller girls start their practice with an exercise. First they'd roll and then fall to the floor and grunt. It was bizarre but interesting. Then they moved on to the actual roller skating part. Nikki jammed into a teammate, who almost fell but managed to stay upright.

It all made me want to come back and watch an actual event. But we were running out of time tonight. I still needed to drop Caleigh off at the agency to get her car, so she could pick up her father.

"Let's go."

We stepped out into the steady roar of L.A.'s early evening traffic.

"Well that was a bust," I said.

"Maybe it's because he's allowed to do it," Caleigh said as we reached my car.

"Come again?"

We settled into our seats. "Men cheat all the time, right? Maybe part of it is because…"

"They're cowards who can't commit or can't tell their significant others that they're not happy?" I interjected.

She chuckled. "Yes, and because it's taboo, and anything we're not supposed to do is more tempting."

I turned the car on and pulled out onto the street.

"Since Stuart's allowed to see other women, since it's almost a requirement of his wife's, maybe he's not interested."

"Maybe." Her logic was flawless, but I didn't like what that meant for us single women who still had a thing for monogamy. Were we doomed to a faithless marriage unless we agreed to an open arrangement? I mean, there had to be some traditional marriages that lasted without cheating. Right?

Too bad I didn't know of any, and my line of business surely didn't help that theory.

Caleigh's phone beeped again. She squealed.

"Good news?" I asked with a chuckle.

She looked up, her eyes lit. "After dinner with Daddy, I have a date with Curtis, the guitar player. We've been texting all day, and he's absolutely yummy and perfect."

"Good for you. But how are you going to go on a date without your fiancé with Daddy around?"

"Simple. I'll just say I'm meeting Danny at his place."

I stopped at the light and flipped on my signal. "Sounds like a plan."

After dinner, I had a date as well, with the ADA. Only he didn't know it.

* * *

I dropped Caleigh off at her car at the agency. She went to get Daddy, while I gathered Maya and Sam, who praised Julio and his great grades on the ride over. She was a proud mama.

Ma Belle's was homey with red and white checkered table cloths, potted plants, and hurricane lamps turned into chandeliers. We arrived and were shown to large table set for five near the back of the restaurant. The hostess said Mr. Presley had called ahead.

The waitress arrived with water served in Mason jars and a basket of homemade biscuits. I'd had a small lunch and was famished. I grabbed a biscuit and sank my teeth in. Flaky, warm, and buttery. I sighed.

I stared at the menu. Everything, well most of it, sounded heavenly. I wasn't very familiar with southern fare, other than cornbread and fried chicken. There seemed to be something for everyone—pork, chicken, beef, seafood, and even a couple of vegetarian dishes.

"Sorry we're late," Caleigh said and sat in the seat across from me. She collapsed into the chair, making it wobble a bit. Her chest rose and fell fast.

I looked up and frowned at the look of panic on her face. What could've possibly happened on the drive over to upset her? "Did you run in here?"

"Yes." She grabbed her glass of water and drank half of it in one gulp.

"Why? Where's your dad?" Maya asked.

"He's coming. I wanted to get in first to warn you." She was looking at me.

My stomach sank again. Oh God. "About what?"

Then I spotted Mr. Presley walking over…beside Danny.

What the hell?

I glared at Caleigh and lowered my voice. "What is he doing here? I thought he wasn't coming."

She shrugged. "He called to say he changed his mind. Something about you needing a bodyguard?"

Was he kidding me?

My glare must've deepened because she quickly said, "He said it jokingly, with laughter."

Right. More likely, he'd taken the opportunity to play this charade with Caleigh in front of me as a way to get back at me for stealing his bug. But it looked like I didn't have a choice but to play along. For Caleigh's sake.

Mr. Presley took the chair at the head of the table between me and Caleigh. Sam sat at the other one, and Maya next to me, which left Danny sitting beside Caleigh and me with ample view of their make-believe hand holding or, heaven forbid, kissing.

He wouldn't take it that far. Would he?

I used my menu to conceal my eye roll. Caleigh was going to owe me many cocktails for tonight.

"Ladies," Danny said, nodding toward Sam and Maya. "Jamie." He turned all 100 watts of his Lady-killer smile on me.

I shot him a death glare back.

If Mr. Presley noticed, he didn't indicate it, instead nodding his hellos all around as he and Danny took their chairs.

"You found a goldmine, Mr. Presley," said Danny, picking up his menu. "I never heard of this restaurant before."

"Please, call me Daddy. You're going to be my son-in-law after all. Part of the family."

I looked up and smiled at Danny. "Yes, you should call him Daddy," I said.

His smile faltered, but he quickly hid his expression in his menu.

The waitress arrived and we ordered. When she gathered the menus and left, Mr. Presley asked, "So tell me, son. What is it about my princess that first attracted you to her?"

Oh I couldn't wait to hear what lie he made up for this. I leaned my elbows on the table, turning my full attention Danny's way.

"The first time I ever saw her, we were on a photo shoot."

That wasn't true. He met Caleigh at the agency, after I'd hired her. He met *me* on a photo shoot. "Really?" I asked, blinking innocently. "Which one?"

"You know, I don't remember," Danny covered easily. Then he added without missing a beat, "But I do remember how gorgeous she looked. She was wearing a hot pink bikini under this gauzy wrap that almost flowed behind her like angel wings."

I coughed, quickly covering it with a sip from my water glass. He was laying it on a bit thick.

"Daddy, I told you that Danny's a photographer," Caleigh quickly jumped in.

"Yes, I remember. Do you still work with pictures?"

"Yes, sir."

That added formality made the corners of Mr. Presley's mouth upturn. "Will its income afford you to support my daughter? It doesn't sound all that stable?"

"Daddy," Caleigh giggled, cutting off any reply Danny was ready to make. "I work too."

He frowned. "For now. Once you're married, you'll want to stay with the babies. Trust me, all women do."

Sam coughed into her napkin. Caleigh kicked her under the table. I seriously needed a drink. Did this place sell moonshine?

Eventually our food arrived. I ordered the crab cake platter, which came with coleslaw, lemon, and tartar sauce. Danny and Mr. Presley both got the brisket with sides of kale and macaroni and cheese. It looked amazing, and if I wasn't still annoyed with him, I'd have taken some off his plate. Well, and if it wasn't for the little fact that I wasn't his pretend girlfriend.

Danny struggled cutting his meat with one arm in a sling. He chuckled as a chunk fell onto the tablecloth. "I thought brisket was supposed to be fork-tender."

Mr. Presley stabbed the air with his fork. "Help him, princess."

Caleigh's eye bounced from me to Danny to the offending piece of meat. "Uh, okay," she said slowly, leaning over her plate to reach her companion's. I watched as she used her knife and fork to cut his meat into bite-sized pieces.

Danny flushed. I wasn't sure if it was because he liked being independent or because Caleigh's position gave him free range of her cleavage. Luckily he turned his head and kept his gaze on the floor until she finished. And that was lucky for him or I'd have to stab *him* with my fork.

When he looked back up our gazes caught. I wished I could've read his expression.

Caleigh finished and patted him on the shoulder.

Daddy frowned.

Caleigh cleared her throat and leaned back toward Danny, giving him the most awkward kiss on the cheek I'd ever witnessed.

Daddy smiled.

I mentally rolled my eyes, shoving a bite of crab cake into my mouth.

Thankfully we fell into a food-induced silence, each of us engrossed—or pretending to be engrossed—in our plates. And it was fine by me. The less talking, the less irritating the night became. But then Mr. Presley cleared his throat, and I held my breath.

"So, Jamie, what made you start a PI business? Surely you're married? You're too beautiful to be single."

Wow, this man clearly lived in a time before even he was born.

Sam opened her mouth to say something, but Caleigh pressed her lips together and gave Sam a stern look.

I spoke up fast. I didn't agree with his idea about women, but this was Caleigh's father. She, at least, deserved respect. "I am not married. I'm very busy with work and haven't had much time for dating."

Danny scoffed. "She also has bad taste in men. Her current crush is on a straight-laced lawyer who has no sense of romance."

"And you do?" I shot back.

Danny chuckled, but his jaw tensed.

Caleigh widened her blue eyes and tried to cover. "He has such a romantic heart."

Mr. Presley hadn't noticed our conversation though. He said, "Ah, lawyers are scum."

Caleigh patted his hand.

To Mr. Presley, I said, "My father started the business. A few years ago, he was injured and needed to step away. I took over."

"I take it your parents have no sons?"

I took a deep breath. "Just me."

He seemed to like that answer, nodding while he chewed. "Children learning the family business is the way it should be."

"So, Mr. Presley, what do you think of L.A. so far?" Danny asked.

"There are a lot of cars."

Danny chuckled. "Most people say smog."

Mr. Presley said, "I figured that was caused by all the cars."

Maya and I giggled. Sam shot us a glare. She was not enjoying her evening.

"So tell me how you hurt your arm, son."

Danny glanced hesitantly to me before speaking. "It was a gun shot."

Mr. Presley frowned, setting down his fork. "Oh, my Lord. How does a photographer get shot?"

"I was helping Jamie and her father with a case."

"It was an accident, Daddy," Caleigh said then turned to Danny and widened her eyes, as if to say he needed to go along with her.

"Yes, that's right. The gun went off accidentally," Danny played along, though his "charming future-son-in-law" act was slipping a little.

When the waitstaff removed our plates and our waitress asked if we'd like dessert, Sam immediately shook her head and said, "No."

Mr. Presley, however, perked up from his food coma and said, "I'd love a piece of pie. It doesn't matter which kind."

Stuck for at least another thirty minutes I leaned back into my seat and glanced at the time on my phone. I hadn't meant for anyone to see the impatient gesture, but no such luck.

"Got somewhere to be tonight, Bond?" Danny asked.

It wasn't so much the question, but the tone—almost mocking as if he didn't believe I would have any evening plans—that spurred me to answer with a, "Actually, yes, I'm seeing someone later."

His smirk faltered for a half a second. "Really? Anyone I know?"

I shrugged. "Just some straight-laced, non-romantic guy." Okay so, it was a small stretch of the truth. Did I plan to *see* Aiden later? Yes. Only it would likely be through my binocular lenses.

Danny's smile was tight, suddenly looking made of plastic. "Well, aren't you the popular girl?" he said. Then he took Caleigh's hand into his, holding it on top of the table. The look in his eye? It was rebellion, as if touching her was his way of saying, "Bring it."

I raised a brow and sipped my coffee. I wasn't going to play his game. If he wanted to tongue Caleigh in front of her father, then that would be fine by me.

Okay, so maybe not *fine*.

Danny jutted his chin down, toward his lap. What the hell…Oh, God, please don't tell me he was trying to hint at some sort of physical attraction happening down below. How crass. How crude. How…honestly unlike Danny.

No matter how deep I frowned though, he kept doing the movement.

I finally shrugged and shook my head. I had no clue.

Aloud he said, "I always find it interesting when people have little habits they repeatedly do when they're stressed or nervous or bothered by something." He put emphasis on the "bothered."

Caleigh laughed like a woman who always chuckled at her husband's jokes, even though they weren't funny.

He squeezed Caleigh's fingers. "A person may deny something is bothering them but that telltale sign suggests otherwise. Like when someone shakes their foot up and down."

What was he blabbering about?

Then I looked down at my lap and realized. I was bouncing my leg. Danny knew I did that when upset.

I looked up, and his grin was a mile wide.

The jerk.

CHAPTER EIGHT

———

Same parking spot, same bat channel. But this time I brought a baggie of green, seedless grapes and trail mix. A little better than Cheetos. I wasn't really hungry after dinner though. They were for just in case the night dragged on into the wee hours.

I zeroed in on Aiden's office, but it was dark, and I couldn't make out any activity on the rest of the floor. He was still in the building though. His car was in the parking lot.

I lowered my binoculars and focused on the front door. If Rocco showed up, I wanted to catch a glimpse of him immediately.

I switched on the radio, but "Love Me Tender" played, so I turned it off. I wanted no more reminders of Daddy Presley. I don't think I'd ever met a more sexist man. Having spent the evening with him, I imagined Caleigh took after her mother. She never talked much about her. Like how I rarely spoke of my mom. I thought about her every day, but I didn't want to share the memories I locked up in my mind. I still missed her too much. Perhaps Caleigh felt the same way.

The building's door moved inward, and suddenly Aiden was in my view, holding it open. I blinked out of my thoughts and focused on the man. Going home so early? He looked to his left, a smile on his face. He was talking to someone. Who…

Miranda, all shiny, dark hair and long legs, stepped out ahead of him. I knew he was a gentleman, but I kinda wished a gust of wind would've forced it out of his grip and hit her in the ass as she passed through.

They walked to the corner. I expected them to stop, say their good nights at an appropriate distance, and to walk in separate directions to their cars. They didn't. She followed him to his car across the parking lot. Maybe she needed to give him a file or they were discussing a case before they parted ways.

No such luck though.

He held open his passenger door and she slithered inside. When his rear lights lit up, and he pulled out of his space, my hand instinctively turned on my ignition. Maybe her car wouldn't start or someone had slashed her tires (now there was a thought!), and Aiden was simply giving her a ride home. He was chivalrous and kind enough to do something so disgusting.

I pulled out onto the street and stayed two car lengths behind them. Tailing 101.

I tried to make out their heads in the dark. Were they talking, laughing, had she placed hers in his lap? The little green monster not only reared its ugly head but roared awake and wanted to bite someone's jugular.

When Aiden turned the next corner, I thought I'd be ill. I watched him pull into a small parking lot beside Franco's.

He did not.

Oh my God, this was a date. When he said he wasn't ready for a relationship, was he really saying he didn't want one with me? Was this his usual spot, where he took all women? Had he been some kind of Romeo all along and I hadn't picked up on it? Was I losing my touch? What a jerk. I wasn't sure if I was more upset with him or myself.

I wanted to hate him, but this crushing sadness weighed on my chest. I thought this was our special place.

I parked across the street, wanting a great view and praying he wouldn't look over and recognize my car as they went inside.

They rounded the corner and Miranda had her arm hooked around Aiden's. Part of me wanted to lay on the horn and scare the crap out of them. They entered the restaurant and the maître d showed them to a cozy table for two by the front windows. Wasn't that where he and I had sat?

My nose tingled as if I was about to start crying, but that was ridiculous because I didn't cry.

I grabbed the binoculars, but it took me a moment to hold them up to my face. I wasn't certain I wanted to see hand holding or other romantic gestures. As if Danny and Caleigh's fake lovey-dovey faces hadn't been nauseating enough tonight, I wasn't sure I could stomach Aiden and Mirada's real ones. But stubborn curiosity got the better of me.

Aiden spoke to the server while Miranda read the menu. The white tablecloths were long, so I couldn't tell if she was playing footsie under the table, but there was a smirk on her face.

The server left, and Aiden turned his attention to her. He probably didn't need to look at the menu. If he brought all his women here, he probably knew it by heart. Friday was chicken marsala, Saturday stuffed shells, and Sunday fettuccine alfredo. So what was Tuesday night?

Betrayal platter with a side of marinara sauce?

My phone rang, and I gladly welcomed the distraction. The caller ID listed a number but the word *private*. "Hello?"

"Jamie?" said a low, raspy voice. I knew immediately who it was. Elaine. Crap.

"Yes."

"It's Elaine. Derek's…friend."

"Hi, how are you?"

She hesitated before answering. "Okay." It was a lie. I heard anxiousness and apprehension in her tone. "I was wondering about your father. Have you spoken with him?"

"Uh, not lately," I said honestly.

She paused. "I thought he was working on a case with you."

Right. Crap. I squeezed my eyes shut and choked out the lie Derek told me to give. "Right, yes, he is. What I meant was he's been hard at work. You know, not really calling all that much. On assignment and all that." Geeze with all the cheating I'd seen in my life, you'd think I'd be better at covering it up.

"Oh." I could hear a million questions in that one word.

"He should be back soon," I told her. I had no idea if it was true or not, but I felt like I had to give her something hopeful to hold onto.

"He's not…I mean…"

"What?"

"It's silly. I don't know why I'd even think this, but I guess I was just sort of worried that maybe he was using this whole story about working for you as a cover. That he was seeing someone else."

Wow. That Elaine was a smart cookie.

"But obviously that's just me being paranoid." She laughed high and loudly in a way that held zero humor.

I suddenly felt like the scum of the earth lying to her. Damn Derek. Damn Aiden, Danny, and all men in general.

Before I could stop myself, I heard my voice saying, "I need a drink. Want to join me, Elaine?"

Elaine and I met at Citylights, a hole in the wall that had cheap cocktails, loyal regulars, and plenty of dark, anonymous booths for drowning your sorrows. Come to find out Elaine didn't live that far from me, and this place was smack dab in the middle. And since she was already closer, I found her waiting at the bar when I walked in. And this place was all bar.

When you walked in, there was a strip of floor that led to either the bar, the jukebox, the restrooms, or a back exit sign. I'd only been in here once. It was about a year ago after an especially long day of stakeouts and spying. My bones were weary, my mind fully alert, and there was no alcohol in my apartment. This had seemed like the best choice.

Tonight it was slow, even for a weekday night.

I sat beside her and ordered a margarita on the rocks.

"You seem to be having as bad a night as I am," she said and sipped her pint glass of very dark beer.

"Very much. But here's to it almost being over."

"So it can start again?" Elaine's sarcasm was thicker than my own.

"Cheers." I clicked my glass against hers and drank a mouthful. I was past the polite and ladylike portion of the evening.

She chuckled. "I thought meeting with my...with Derek's daughter would be intimidating."

I almost choked on my drink. "Why?"

"You're beautiful. I remember seeing you on the covers of *Sport's Illustrated* and *Vogue*. But you're actually down-to-earth."

I smiled. Everyone always had preconceived notions about models. They assumed we were all anorexic and survived on soda crackers, celery, and diet soda, or that we were dumb. I could throw down a cheeseburger with the burliest of men. And while I didn't have a PhD, I ran a successful business and drove a killer car.

"Derek said you weren't stuck up, but seeing how he's your dad, I wasn't sure if he was biased," Elaine said.

The last conversation I wanted to have tonight was about the two of them. I couldn't deal with another man. "Let's not talk about Derek tonight. Is that okay?"

She smiled. "Yes, that's great. So how's work?"

If we discussed the agency, we'd sooner or later hit the topic of Derek, so I steered the conversation to safer grounds. "It's fine. But what about you? Do you like working at the station?"

I'd first encountered Elaine when Derek had directed us to one of his "special friends" at Channel Four in conjunction with another case.

"It's okay. The hours are fine. Pay is okay. That could always be better. I wouldn't mind finding something a bit more adventurous though. Not quite being a PI, but not answering phones either," she said. "I'm not sure what though. Did you always want to be a model?"

"Actually I never considered it before I was approached by an agent. At first I thought of being an actress. Growing up in L.A., the idea of making it into Hollywood is everywhere."

Looking back now, I realized acting was a part of my career choices—not that the second career had been much of a choice. I couldn't say no to Derek because he was family. If I had to do it all over again though, I'd end up exactly where I was. I loved modeling, but I was glad it didn't have a long shelf-life. And now, being a private investigator was pretty rad. I was a bit disillusioned at first, with the number of cheating spouses in L.A., but in our own special way, the agency helped people. That made up for it.

"What about you?" I asked.

She sipped her drink then laughed. Loud. "I don't exactly have the look Hollywood prefers."

Elaine was small in height and rather large in the chest. The double D's might have been a selling point to casting agents, but the three-packs-a-day smoker's voice was not.

As if she could read my thoughts, she reached into her bag and pulled out a pack of Marlboros. Since she wasn't legally allowed to smoke in a public place, even a bar, she just tapped the pack on the counter several times.

"What did you dream of doing?" I asked, bringing my glass to my lips again.

"Well that's just it. I didn't have any true dreams, the ones of becoming famous or rich. I grew up in Chicago with a single mom. It was rough at times. I assumed I'd get a job waiting tables, like her, or maybe go to nursing school."

"But you didn't?"

She shook her head. "No. I fell in love and followed the boy to L.A. How original, right?"

I smiled. "It happens. Love is a powerful thing."

We both slipped into a melancholic haze. I snapped out of it fast though. I couldn't afford to wallow about Aiden, and I wasn't talking about Derek.

"You decided to stay here though. You didn't want to return home?"

She snapped her fingers at the bartender and pointed to our glasses. Hers was empty, but I still had half a drink left. "By the time he and I split, Mom had passed away."

"I'm sorry. I lost my mother young, too." There we were slipping down that Derek slope again. Was there no way to avoid him?

"And L.A. is home for me, too. I love it here. I never want to leave. Although I wouldn't mind traveling."

"Where would you like to go?"

The bartender set two more drinks down, and Elaine fished a twenty from her wallet. "My treat. No argument."

I only smiled. A free drink was close to a free meal in my book.

"Paris definitely. And Rome, London, Madrid…the popular places, but I don't want to go as a tourist and see the attractions. I want to see what the locals do."

"So you'll need a local guide for each city. A hot Italian and Frenchman and so on," I said, starting to loosen up and feel relaxed.

She leaned closer. "Are there any hot Frenchmen?"

I had to think about that. "Michael Vartan from *Alias*."

Her eyes widened. "The boyfriend?"

I nodded.

"Oooh, oui."

We laughed and continued dishing about hot men of all nationalities. We stayed away from the topic of any real men in our lives, and by the end of the night, or the early hours of the next day, I was glad I'd opted for margaritas with Elaine versus torturing myself about Franco's. She was a nice lady. She deserved great things.

And if Derek really was cheating on her, I was gonna kill him.

CHAPTER NINE

———

"Here you go, boss." Maya handed me the printed-out photos I took of the car shop thugs. "The three of them, Cortez, Alvarez, and Santos, are affiliated in one way or another with an arm of the Mexican mafia. The crew of a man named Eduardo Vega."

Mexican mafia? That was more than a low-level guy in Inglewood who sold to strippers.

But before I could respond, the main door opened, and Caleigh and her father walked in. A sigh escaped before I could stop it.

"Well good morning, ladies." Mr. Presley tipped his hat at us before taking it off and holding it at his chest. "I understand why my princess enjoys L.A. so much. The weather is gorgeous."

Caleigh squeezed his arm. "Daddy and I had an early breakfast." Her smile was forced.

"She introduced me to Who-vos Ran-cher-ous."

Maya and I blinked at him.

"Huevos Rancheros," Caleigh translated.

He held a hand over his belly. "It was a bit spicy. I hope my system can handle it. But it was very delicious. I hadn't realized I'd be eating foreign foods when I came to California."

I was proud of myself that I resisted the giant eye roll just begging to accompany his statement.

He widened his blue eyes. "I'd like to apologize to you lovely ladies, as well as Miss Cross, if I came across as stuffy last night. My daughter seems to think I offended y'all with my talk of women in the home and having babies."

Maya and I looked at one another not sure how to agree without coming across as rude.

Luckily he kept talking and wasn't looking for a response. "I was born in a time when that was normal. Sometimes it's hard to change your thoughts when the world changes. I meant no disrespect."

He seemed like a nice man, and he loved his daughter, wanted the best for her. I decided to cut him some slack.

I stepped forward and took his hand. "Thank you, Mr. Presley. That means a lot to us. It's hard living in a man's world."

I hadn't exactly meant that the way he obviously took it, but when he smiled and squeezed my hand, correcting his assumption didn't matter.

"And thank you for dinner," Maya said.

"It was my pleasure, darlin'. Not only did I get to meet my future son-in-law, but I got to spend time with the people who mean the most to my baby. I call that a win-win."

"Daddy, why don't you go wait in my office. I need to go over some work stuff with Jamie and Maya."

"Okay, pumpkin'. Ladies." He walked off.

"So anything new come up overnight that I need to help with?"

I shook my head. "No."

"Okay, well, I'm going to send Daddy back to my place and then check in with what Stuart Livingston is up to. Maybe he'll meet up with Nikki or Melanie for an afternoon quickie."

I wished. "This afternoon we're going to meet with girlfriend number three."

"But enough about business," Maya interjected. "Tell us about your night."

I had to admit, after the evening I'd had, it would be refreshing to hear about a successful date.

"Well, I dropped Daddy off at my place then pretended Danny and I wanted to be alone. I took him home, and then I met up with Curtis."

"Did he say anything about me?" I asked, hoping I'd hit a nerve with Danny with my fake Aiden meeting.

Caleigh wrinkled her nose. "Why would Curtis talk about you? He hasn't even met you. Well, you were there when we met, but you didn't introduce yourselves to one another. And…"

"Not him. Danny."

She giggled. "Oh. Let's see. He sat in my passenger seat and stared out the window and mumbled about tough brisket, fork-tender crab cakes, and needing a drink."

I smirked. Perhaps it was in bad taste, but I was glad to know last night wasn't uncomfortable just for me.

"He asked me if you had plans to go back to Ventura's today."

I stiffened. "Oh really?"

She cut the air with her hand, like a horizontal karate chop. "I told him absolutely not. Are you?"

I laughed. "I don't think so."

"Whew. I hate lying."

I cocked my head toward her office.

She rolled her eyes. "Yes, I know. It's killing me."

I didn't ask when she'd tell her father the truth, but eventually she'd have to tell some version. Unless, of course, she actually planned on marrying Danny.

She went to her office as the phone rang, and Maya answered it.

I sipped the coffee Maya had waiting for me. I needed it. After my night of cocktails with Elaine, I'd finally slept soundly, only to be woken extra early by an incessant car alarm on the street and then a couple fighting next door.

Sam walked in, out of breath. Her normally curly hair looked frizzy and in need of hydration. Her blouse was wrinkled, and her left shoe looked freshly scuffed.

"What happened to you?" I asked.

"Julio and I overslept. We had to rush to get him to school on time. He hates when he's tardy."

"Late night?"

"After dinner with *that man* I may have had a drink or two." Sam had clearly been the most annoyed by Daddy's comments.

I filled her in on Mr. Presley's apology.

She un-pursed her lips. "Well that was nice of him. I'll be in my office trying to get a grape jelly stain out of my skirt." She pointed to a spot near her hip then walked off.

Maya finally hung up, and I said, "Back to Vega. Are there any big cases coming up involving his crew?"

"Yes. Vega's second in command, a man named Jose Flores, was busted on a DUI. They found drugs in his car, and he's looking at a hefty sentence."

"So Rocco is probably a low level guy sent by Vega to hand off the bribe money to someone in the DA's office." The question was, who was he paying?

"Who's trying the case?"

Maya looked up with wide eyes. Her lips were pursed. "You're not going to like it."

My stomach dropped. These little warnings about my not liking something were starting to wear thin. Maybe the girls just needed to surprise me. Before Maya said anything though, I knew.

"It's Aiden."

No. I couldn't believe Aiden would do that…would he? But how well did I really know him? Maybe the "Golden Boy" act he had going on really was just an act. It was hard to wrap my head around. I didn't want to believe that, but then I envisioned him and Miranda sitting cozy at our restaurant. Although it wasn't really ours anymore.

One thing was for sure—I needed answers.

* * *

Sam and I headed back to Vanessa's house. Clipboard in hand, we walked up the broken concrete and knocked on her door. This time the curtains were drawn, so I couldn't see inside. After yesterday's fiasco at Ventura's, I just hoped Rocco didn't answer. The Toyota was the only car near the house, in the same spot as yesterday.

The door swung open, and Vanessa's smile instantly turned sour at the sight of us. "What do you want?" Her tone was anything but welcoming.

"We have a few more questions about…"

"No. I spoke to Rocco. He said I do not have to answer your questions. This is harassment, and I am done talking." She folded her arms across her chest.

She had us. Once she clammed up, there was no other place to get answers.

As much as it reeked, I decided to go with plan B. "Well, Rocco is wrong. When it comes to the safety and welfare of your children, we have every right to ask whatever we want. We also have every right to do what is best for them, if we determine there is just cause."

She just glared at me, not even tempted to start talking.

Fine. I glanced at Sam before saying, "And the CPS office is starting proceedings to have the children removed from your home."

Vanessa's eyes darkened, and her face flushed. She threw her hands up and yelled something in Spanish. "Go. Leave. You will not take my kids. I'm a good mother. Get out. And don't come back."

Then she took a step back and slammed the door in our faces.

That went well.

Sam raised her brows to me as we turned and headed back to my car.

"Don't give me that look. I remember what you said last time. I didn't want to do it, but I had to."

I opened my car door and slipped in behind the wheel.

She settled in then turned to me. "Okay, I give. Why?" Sam asked.

"Where do you think is the first place Rocco will turn for help with his kids' case?"

Sam grinned. "His contact in the DA's office."

"Bingo."

I turned on the ignition.

"So, you've been spying on Aiden every night?"

She made it sound so immoral. I turned at the corner and headed back to the office. "Not Aiden specifically. The whole office."

"How's that going?" I wasn't sure but I think I detected a note of sarcasm.

I shrugged, not wanting to repeat last night's fiasco. Living through it had been bad enough.

"That good, huh?"

Oh yeah, definitely some sarcasm. Thing was, I knew her concern was legit. Staking out the DA's office every night had started taking its toll on me. Not to mention sitting in the car.

"How about you let me run surveillance tonight?"

I glanced her way. It was like this woman could read my mind. "You sure?"

"Absolutely. Julio has a sleepover, and I'll just be watching some reality show anyway. Might as well make it the real thing."

"Thanks. That's great. I could use the rest."

Actually, I just wasn't sure if I could take watching Aiden and Hot Lips Miranda go out again.

CHAPTER TEN

———

That afternoon, Caleigh and I went to visit Livingston's third girlfriend, Marguerite Clemens. I pulled my roadster up to a wrought iron gate and pressed a button on the talk box of her Beverly Hills home. From the look of the neighborhood, Marguerite had money and plenty of it. Maya's research had pulled up that she was a fifty-seven year-old woman who never worked a day in her life. She'd gone through three husbands, and added a new wing to the house after each one.

"Stuart has great taste," Caleigh whispered from the passenger seat.

I chuckled. "You haven't seen her yet."

She waved a hand along our view. "Do I have to?"

The box crackled to life. "May I help you?"

I stifled a laugh and leaned out my window. "It's Jamie Bond and Caleigh Presley to see Ms. Clemens."

The gate slowly opened without another word.

I drove along the circular driveway, past the immaculate lawn and square-shaped shrubbery, up to a long, stone staircase that led to double glass and gold doors. Well, not actual gold…at least I didn't think it was real, but with some rich people, you never knew.

As we walked up the stairs, the front door opened, and a woman looking slightly younger than her years stepped out. She had thick, light auburn hair that fell in waves around her shoulders. Hazel eyes lined in a smoky, gray liner, full lips from too much collagen moistened with a pink-tinted gloss, and a smattering of freckles that spread out across her neck and chest.

She wore a tight, dark brown skirt that fell a good inch-and-a-half above her knees and a leopard blouse with a deep-V that showed off her very high, very bouncy tatas. A thin gold belt with matching, five-inch heels completed the look. Despite the cliché cougar wardrobe, she was absolutely stunning.

She held up a finger adorned in an emerald ring the size of a walnut. "Don't tell me." She pointed to me, stared at my face, then did the same to Caleigh. "You are Miss Presley."

Caleigh's eyes lit up. "Yes. How'd you know?"

"You have the same chin as the King."

Caleigh squealed. "I do. No one's ever noticed that before." She gave me a see-I-told-you look.

"Well, let's not stand out here in the sun. It wreaks havoc on the skin," Marguerite said then wrapped an arm around Caleigh's shoulders and led her inside.

Did she always welcome strangers so easily into her home?

I followed and tried not to gawk at the statue of a naked man, anatomy ridiculously accurate, in the foyer beside a winding staircase.

But Marguerite must've caught my eye because she whistled and said, "Gorgeous, isn't he? It just arrived this morning, and I'm not sure where to put him. At first I thought the sunroom, but now I'm thinking my bedroom."

Yes, because that's what I wanted to see when I woke in the middle of the night, just standing there—his penis pointing at me in the dark.

She led the way into a sitting room and waved her hand. "Please take a seat. Would you like coffee, tea, whiskey? I can have the girl bring it to us."

"No, thank you," I said and sat on the edge of a brown suede sectional.

Caleigh sat beside me, but she leaned back against the cushions, making herself comfortable. "The girl?"

Marguerite sat opposite us, on a bright red chair, the only item in the room that wasn't brown, gold, or off-white. "Please forgive my tackiness. Every month for the past eight, the cook has quit. Just poof, up and left like a bad magician's vanishing act. I can no longer keep track of names."

"Why have they quit?" I asked, curious to how the other half lived.

"The last one said I'm too demanding. I don't see how breakfast in bed is demanding when I pay her handsomely."

"That's it? Breakfast in bed?" Caleigh asked.

Marguerite giggled. "She may have walked in on me and a male guest in a compromising position as it was delivered. Let's just say my friend is as endowed as my statue."

I shifted in my seat and felt Caleigh stifle a giggle beside me.

Marguerite smiled. "Exactly. Now, what can I do for you beautiful young women?"

As I opened my mouth, she winked and whispered, "Love your shoes."

I glanced down at my pink pumps and grinned. "Thank you. I, um…we're here because you know Stuart Livingston."

She wiggled her eyebrows. "Do I ever. Is he okay?"

"He's fine. Have you seen him recently?"

"Sadly, I have not. Stuart is an old soul. He's gentle, wise, and very passionate. I'm not just talking romantically either. He cares deeply about things. Animals, wild life, our environment. That man knows more about marine biology than my old professor in college."

"When was the last time you met with him?" I asked.

"Oh, it's been a few weeks. I miss him terribly too. He is…"

"Yeah. We know," I stopped her. "He's great in bed."

I looked to Caleigh and sighed. Kate was right. Somehow she was married to the one faithful man in L.A.

We sat there for another hour as she told us all about meeting Stuart, her love of art, especially paintings and statues of naked men, and her childhood dream of being a pianist, even though she never learned to play. I learned more about her childhood than I remembered of my own. She loved to talk and had a way with words that made it difficult to interject.

Finally I managed to ask, "How did Stuart seem the last time you saw him?"

"Quiet. But that wasn't odd. He was always talking about his wife and how much he loved her. It should have bothered me, but it was so cute and endearing, I didn't mind. Plus, he was really great in bed."

I rose, and Caleigh followed. "We should get going. Thank you so much for taking the time to meet with us."

She showed us to the door. "It was my pleasure, dears. Any time you're in the neighborhood and want to chat, just stop by. I know some men who would make your hair curl."

I expected Caleigh to laugh or purr in typically adorable Caleigh style, but she just waved good-bye.

As we settled into my car, I asked, "What's wrong with you?"

She widened her eyes. "What do you mean?"

I pulled out of the gate and hung a right. "You didn't react to her mention of hot, single guys."

She giggled. "I'm a one-man kind of girl now."

I raised an eyebrow at her. "Curtis?"

She nodded. "He is absolutely amazing. He's totally romantic. We went for a picnic on the beach last night. The moon, the water, a bottle of wine. I think it's love."

"That's great, Caleigh." I was glad at least someone's love life was happening and happy.

My phone rang. I pulled it from my purse, wedged between the two front seats. "Hello?"

"James. Has Elaine talked to you?" It was Derek.

"Yeah, we had drinks together last night."

"Is she okay?" He sounded tense.

"As okay as she can be considering her boyfriend is lying to her."

He sighed. "I'll be a few days longer than I thought."

I hung a left on Wilshire. "What are you doing?"

"It's personal." The line clicked in my ear.

Damn man. Just as I was about to set the phone in my purse, it rang again. I swiped the on button. "Did we get disconnected, or did you hang up on me on purpose?"

"It's Danny." His tone was rough and tight.

"Oh. Hi, I—" I glanced at the time. Four-twenty. Shoot.

"You forgot to pick me up."

"I'm so sorry. I was with a client, and the time got away. Are you still waiting?"

"No, I took a cab home."

My guilt rose. First our fight, then that weird dinner, and now this. "I'll make it up to you."

"Oh yeah? How?" The annoyance seemed to subside, and in its place was intrigue mixed with playfulness in his voice. When you spent a good portion of your life listening to others, you tended to pick up on tones easily.

"I'll...make you dinner," I grasped. "Tonight."

"You're gonna cook?"

"Dinner at your place at seven. Don't make plans."

"You got it, Bond."

"See you later," I said then hung up.

"Who was that?" Caleigh asked with a snicker.

I smiled. "Your fiancé."

CHAPTER ELEVEN

———

When I said I'd cook, what I really meant was that I'd buy dinner from one of my favorite restaurants and bring it to his apartment. When he opened the door, I held up two bags of deliciousness from Chez Robert.

"This is cooking?" He smirked.

"Yep."

He opened the door wider, and I noticed he wore a pair of well-worn jeans and a black polo shirt, both of which clung to his fit physique in a way that had me imagining he could pose for one of Marguerite's statues. And when I passed him, I caught a whiff of soap and heady musk from his aftershave. Damn, he smelled better than the food.

I walked farther into the living room and realized he'd changed things. Where there was once a sofa, coffee table, a TV, and dumbbells, now there was the addition of an area rug, an armchair, a cactus plant on a side table, a couple of lamps, and framed photos of various location shots on the wall. The photos were his own work, from places I knew he'd been over the years, enlarged and framed. They looked amazing. His apartment looked homey. Could it be that Loverboy was becoming domesticated?

I entered the kitchen and set the bags on the counter. Danny helped me take the trays of food out and open them.

"This looks great," he said while lifting the lid off garlic mashed potatoes. When he got to the filet mignon, I heard him sigh.

I smiled, pleased. "I forgot beverages. I hope you have something, or I can run back out real quick."

He opened a cabinet and pulled out a bottle of wine. "For special occasions."

I assumed he'd have beer. This was ten times better.

While he uncorked the top and got glasses, I took out a couple of his dishes and plated the food.

"Should I cut your steak for you?" I asked with a smirk. I said it jokingly, a jab about last night, but at the same time, I was also serious. I had asked the restaurant to slice it rather than serving up a giant slab of cow, but I still wasn't totally sure he could manage.

"Haha, you're funny." But he eyed the meat and must've been satisfied with the size. "It's fine. Plus it actually looks tender."

"Yeah, what was up with the brisket needing a blow torch?"

My exaggeration made him laugh.

We brought everything into his small dining area and sat at the square table.

He held up his glass of wine. "To friends."

I clinked my glass against his and took a sip. The aromatic flavor coated my tongue. It was nice to relax during a good meal. "So, last night…" I began.

He glanced up, held my gaze, waited for me to finish. When I didn't, he added, "It was awkward."

I laughed. "Yeah. Caleigh's dad is old-fashioned. No progressive parenting there."

I knew I had to apologize for my quick temper yesterday afternoon, but I feared that if it was only one-sided, I'd get annoyed again. The last thing I wanted was to tarnish this evening. It was the most relaxed I'd been all week.

Danny smiled. "This food is delicious. Last night, yesterday is…well, over."

In other words, we didn't need to dwell and talk things to death. Being friends with Danny was easy.

As I cut into my steak (It was fork-tender, so whew.), I glanced to a side table he'd added to this part of the room. On it were a couple of framed photos. One was of three boys. They smiled into the camera with their arms around each other's shoulders. The middle one had a wicked, familiar grin.

"Is that you?"

Danny followed my gaze and nodded. "Yep. I was ten."

I set down my fork and reached for the picture. The boy on his right was dark-skinned and bald, or very closely shaved, and the other boy had short black hair and a toothless grin. He was younger than the others.

"Who are they?"

"My brothers." Danny bit into a roll.

Brothers? I quirked a brow. "Um, how do you have a black and an Asian brother? Unless you were adopted."

"Yeah."

Wait. What? "You were adopted? Why don't I know this?"

He winked. "I told you, you don't know everything about me. And I wasn't exactly adopted. I lived in foster care. They're Charlie and Eugene, my foster brothers."

I'd heard him mention those names before, but I assumed they were just old high school buddies. I hadn't a clue Danny spent time in the system. And here I spent countless hours complaining to him about Derek and grieving about my dead mom…and I knew nothing about his childhood. What kind of friend was I?

"So tell me about it. How long were you with them? Where are your biological parents? Everything."

He opened his mouth to speak, and I held up a hand. "Wait. First, why haven't you mentioned this before?"

He shrugged and swallowed a piece of meat. "It's not something you go around saying."

I leaned forward and touched his hand. "Danny, I've know you for a million years. I'm your best friend." Or at least I assumed I was. Please don't let it be that I misread another person in my life.

He squeezed my fingers. "It's not you. It's just…not something I talk about. With anyone."

I could tell I'd hit an emotional nerve. Danny didn't do emotional. Neither did I usually.

I pulled back and stabbed my fork into my asparagus. "I understand. If you don't want to talk about it, that's fine." And it was, but I had so many questions. I didn't want to pry though. I did that all day, every day at work. I just wanted a relaxing evening with a friend…with this friend.

"My mom was fifteen when she had me," he said, while pushing a clump of potatoes around his plate.

I continued to eat, not wanting to interrupt, hoping he'd reveal all.

"She and her family were Catholic, so going through with the pregnancy was her only option, but her folks forced her to give me up." He looked up. "I haven't met her face-to-face. Maybe some day. But we exchanged letters a few years ago. Around the time you came home."

I sucked in a breath. So while Derek had been shot and I was taking over the Bond Agency, Danny had been dealing with his bio mom and never said a word. If I hadn't had so much on my plate, I could've helped him with what he was going through. That timing sucked. Of course it wasn't my fault, but I still felt guilty.

"I grew up in the system," he continued. "At first I was adopted by a great couple, or so I'm told. I don't remember them much. The wife died when I was five, of cancer. The husband was devastated. He started drinking, couldn't deal, and couldn't take care of me. He gave me back." Danny chuckled, but from its rough tone, it was anything funny.

A wedge of steak got stuck in my throat. I took a gulp of wine and swallowed. "It's good you don't remember them then."

He nodded and scooped up a forkful of potatoes. "This is so good."

"Yeah, they use just the right amount of garlic and fresh chives."

We ate for a few minutes in silence. I figured that was all he wanted to share, until he said, "I grew up in foster care after that. I'd been bounced around to three different homes before the Reynolds took me in."

He thrust his fork toward the photo I placed on the table. "That's where I met Charlie and Eugene. I was there from ten until I graduated high school. They were a good family. Had a huge old farmhouse and a couple of cows."

I nearly dropped my wine glass. "You grew up in the country?"

He laughed, genuinely. "Not exactly. The cows weren't there long, but if we're ever stranded on a farm and thirsty." He fist bumped his chest. "I can get us some milk."

I giggled, imagining Danny squatting by udders. "You've kept in touch with your brothers. How about your foster parents?"

"Mrs. Reynolds still lives in that house, still taking in kids when she can. Mr. Reynolds died about five years ago. Heart attack." He smiled to himself, as if he'd just conjured a great memory. "They were…are good people. I try to visit when I can, but I've traveled so much, I don't get as much time as I would've liked."

"So what drew you to photography?" I bit into an asparagus spear.

"In tenth grade I took a class in school. I was hooked. But I always knew I wanted to travel, to see the world. A nine-to-five never appealed to me. The same town, same bed, same routine. I was never good with stagnant, repetitions. It led to boredom…and eventually good-byes."

And there it was. Danny's sense of adventure, his need to serial date, it was due to his upbringing. Not being able to count on the very people who raised him. It was as if a curtain was drawn back. How everything about him suddenly made so much sense. In hindsight, I almost felt stupid for not realizing there had been a reason to begin with.

"And now?" I asked. "You've been in this apartment for three years. Haven't left the country in about that long. What's changed?"

He looked up, stared into my eyes. A smile tugged one corner of his mouth. "I like what's here. It's worth sticking around."

A warm sensation fluttered in my belly.

After we finished eating, I wrapped up the leftovers and put them in Danny's fridge. As I wiped down his table, he walked into the room with a photo album. "I have more pictures if you're interested."

"Of course I am." I pulled my chair around toward his and sat down.

He flipped open the book. The first page held four Polaroids held down by those old-fashioned corner tabs. Each picture held a toothless, grinning infant. He was a happy baby, despite his circumstances.

"These are the only ones I have from when I lived with my first family."

While the photos were adorable, the fact that he didn't have more of his childhood saddened me. I no longer possessed items that reminded me of my mother, but I still had my memories. Danny didn't even have those.

He flipped the page. There was Danny on a rocking horse, Danny by a pumpkin almost the size of him, and Danny crying on Santa Claus's lap. He had to be around six or seven.

"That beard scared the crap out of me."

I giggled. We looked through the rest of the book. He pointed out various adventures with Charlie and Eugene. The Reynolds had a treehouse in their yard, and most of the photos were taken up there. There were also some of them with their foster parents—two proud, stocky people with their arms around the kids. At least Danny grew up in a happy home. Some kids didn't get that.

We took our glasses and the bottle of wine and sat on the couch. A small light above his stove seeped into the living room, but no other lights were on. I shut my eyes for a moment, just breathing in the silence. My body was heavy and comfortable, like I could nap.

Then Danny's fingers found their way to my arm. He moved them up and down, caressing my skin in the subtlest motions.

Suddenly, the desire to kick off my shoes and find a blanket disappeared. Every nerve ending was charged, awake, and Danny's fingertips left a blazing trail. Sensations flooded my lower belly, and I sighed.

I wanted to lean into him, press myself against him. I wanted to feel his hands along my body, his mouth on mine.

Danny turned toward me, and even in the dim light I could see the same hunger in his eyes...

A breath strangled in my throat, and I jumped off the couch. What the hell was I doing? This was Danny, my best friend. If anything happened that friendship would be gone, and then what? I didn't know if I truly wanted this or if it was just the moment. I couldn't risk ruining everything.

"What's wrong?" he asked.

I switched on a lamp and gave an uneven chuckle. "I just remembered I have more work to do tonight."

Danny frowned. "What kind of work? Is this about that chop-shop again?"

"What? No. Kinda of." My tongue was suddenly as confused as my hormones.

"I'll come with you."

"No! It's, uh, just paperwork. At the office. Boring stuff. I need to run, but I won't forget about therapy tomorrow."

As I ran from his apartment, I knew I'd made a mistake. But I wasn't sure if the mistake was almost kissing him or leaving.

* * *

Of course, I didn't end up at the office. At least not mine. Instead I needed to torture myself and park outside the DA's office again. I pulled up beside Sam's car then got out and into her passenger seat.

"What are you doing here?" she asked, a look of surprise on her face.

"I needed distraction."

Sam dusted cookie crumbs off her jeans. From the array of empty packages of snack foods, it looked like she enjoyed the same stakeout delicacies as I did.

"Is the reason you didn't get dessert at the restaurant last night because you had a stockpile of Hostess cakes in your car?"

She looked down to the wrappers and chuckled. "No, Julio keeps leaving them in here. I'm not sure why. And refusing dessert last night was so I could get out of there. I love Caleigh but not so much her dad."

Yeah, it hadn't been a fun evening for me either.

"And I thought my father was overbearing," she said. "At least he worked around some amazing military women and knew we didn't just belong in an apron."

I stared at her profile. Her jaw was clenched, her eyes narrowed. "This really bothers you."

She was silent for a moment. Then she nodded and let out a half-laugh. "I guess more than I thought. So tell me, how did tonight go?"

"Good." I focused on what I learned about Danny and his foster family and refused to think about the end, the feelings that still coursed through me.

Sam stared at me with that look like she knew I was holding back.

I quickly changed the subject before she questioned it. I could keep things from Caleigh and Maya without much thought, but Sam, for some reason, seemed to always pull things out of me. I swore it was a secret ability she wasn't sharing.

"How's it going here?"

"So far nothing. No one in or out, and no sign of Rocco."

Of course. Was it too much for the Universe to lend a hand?

"What about Aiden and Miranda?" Saying her name left a bitter coating on my tongue.

Sam shook her head. "Not much from him either. He was at his desk working earlier. I don't know where he went off to. He hasn't been at his desk for a good twenty minutes, but he hasn't left yet either. I haven't seen her at all."

Good. Was it possible Miranda left work at a normal hour tonight and was home taking a bath, mending her black, pointy hat, polishing her broom?

"Okay, well, I'll take over. Go home and enjoy some late night reality TV," I said.

"You sure? I have enough sugar in me to last a couple more hours."

I chuckled, opened the car door, and stepped out. "Absolutely."

"Have a good night," she said and started her engine.

I went back to my car, waved as she drove off, then pulled up into the spot she had vacated. I pulled my binoculars from my backseat and leaned back in my seat.

The light in Aiden's office was on, but there was no movement. No Aiden, no Miranda, just like Sam had said. Thank goodness. I couldn't stomach Miranda latching onto him tonight.

Movement caught my eye, and I lowered the binoculars to the front door.

Thank you, Universe.

Sure enough there was Rocco entering the building.

Without a thought, I raced across the street and straight to the stairs, knowing he'd take the elevator. A weird sense of déjà vu overcame me as I hiked up my skirt and ran up three flights. This time I wasn't panting nearly as hard. (I'd done a load of laundry the other night, so I wore a pink lacy thong. Not necessarily better in this case.)

As I scrambled through the floor doors, I pushed my skirt down. Rocco stood in the same spot as last time. Instead of getting on all fours again, I turned the corner, and pressed myself against the wall. I counted to five and then peeked. And waited.

He walked down the back hall, and I followed.

Like before, he entered the DA's office.

I ran on tippy toes and pressed my ear against the door.

Muffled voices sounded, but I couldn't make out who they belonged to. But there were definitely two people inside.

I thought of the ajar office door, the one Miranda had walked through the other night, and I stepped farther down the hall, wanting to find that room. The next door was unmarked. I gripped the knob and turned. It wasn't locked. I eased it open gently, holding my breath. Hopefully I wouldn't walk in on someone at their desk, like Miranda.

It was an office, but it was dark and empty. From the hallway light that spilled in, I'd say it belonged to an assistant. A silver photo frame sat on the windowsill, with the picture of a fat, smiling baby.

I shut the door then walked to the adjoining one. It was open a crack, just enough to make out the voices.

"But what if they come back and take the kids away?" asked a man with a heavy Hispanic accent. Rocco.

Good, my plan had worked. Vanessa was scared, and he came running. Not that I wanted her to fear her children's safety, but luckily it was all fear and no action.

"I'll look into it."
I froze. The second voice was one I knew very well.
Rocco was meeting with Aiden.

CHAPTER TWELVE

Suddenly everything I thought I knew about Aiden turned on its head. If I hadn't heard him with my own ears, I never would've believed he was conspiring with a drug dealer. How could I have been so stupid? Believing he wore the white hat, combating injustice for the people. Ha!

And if the good-guy routine wasn't real...had any of it been real? Had he been using me for...something? I was drawing a blank on what for, but if I was given time I was sure I'd learn the truth about that too.

My knees trembled, and I wasn't sure if it was because I'd been played and felt like a fool, or because I was seething with anger. How could I have let this happen? Why was I so blind?

But even as I stood there listening and replaying every word and touch Aiden and I had shared, from our first encounter at a fundraiser to the night on my steps when he pushed me away, nothing made sense.

The men said their good-byes.

I pressed myself against the wall, praying neither would come this way. The DA's hall door opened. I ran to the assistant's door and opened it just in time to see them both leave the office. Rocco walked toward the elevator, while Aiden turned around and headed toward me.

I sprang back and considered hiding under the desk, but then I remembered his office was just a couple of doors down. He had no reason to come in here.

I peeked out again and caught the hem of his jacket going into his own office.

But before I had time to contemplate my next move, Aiden was back in the hall with his briefcase in hand. He was leaving. I sucked in a breath as he walked past me.

I hurried to the windows and bent a blind to peer out. My car was parked almost directly across from where I stood. Hopefully Aiden wouldn't see it when he left. I couldn't make out the parking lot from my position, but when his car pulled out, I'd see it.

It took longer than I expected, maybe because I tapped my foot to every second that passed. He hung a right out of the lot, not slowing down, which I hoped meant he hadn't noticed my car.

I stood back, listened to the silence, and smiled. I was alone in the building. Well, maybe not completely. There were probably janitors and a few other scattered workers. But if Aiden wasn't here, that meant I could snoop in his office, find proof that he was taking bribes without the risk of being caught by him. I couldn't have planned a more perfect opportunity if I had tried.

I slipped out of the assistant's office and into Aiden's without being noticed. Did no one lock doors in this building? How could the DA's office be so trusting? It didn't make sense. They wouldn't take the risk. This entire floor should've been on lockdown. Obviously someone left the downstairs door unlocked so Rocco could come and go, but why hadn't anyone else noticed that? And why was the interior so freely accessed? The DA's own office? It was more a conference room for criminals than anything else.

I immediately went to Aiden's desk and sat in his chair. I took a moment to breathe in his musky scent. Deceived or not by who he was, it still smelled warm and familiar.

On the corner of his desk was a framed photo of him and a woman. His late wife. I picked it up and examined it closer. I'd never actually seen her before. She'd been pretty. Blonde, shoulder length hair blowing in the breeze, smiling blue eyes, a thin nose, and full lips. They looked happy. A clear blue sky was in the background. It was a close-up, so I couldn't tell where they were. Maybe a tropical beach on their honeymoon. I could only make out the wide shoulder straps. It could've been the top of a dress or a tank with shorts.

Did I remind him of her? When he gazed into my eyes, was he seeing her or me?

I set the picture back and combed through the drawers and the file cabinet (Which was locked, but I easily found a key in a drawer. So really, why bother?). It took me about thirty minutes to go through every inch of his office, and unfortunately, or fortunately, I found nothing incriminating.

As I was about to leave, I remembered the bug Danny had dropped into my purse. I fished it out from the bottom of my bag, beneath a bottle of hand sanitizer, a compact, and a half-eaten roll of Rolos. Oooh, I'd forgotten those were in there.

I glanced around the room, wondering about the best spot, but there were no plants or vases to slip it into. Instead, I had to make do with placing it on a shelf, behind a framed photo of Aiden, the DA, and the Mayor during some award ceremony. They looked chummy.

Satisfied Aiden wouldn't notice it, I walked out, slipped down the hall like a ninja, and made it outside without being seen. I was great at this spy business.

When I stepped into my apartment, I kicked off my heels and noticed a message on my phone. I played it.

"Jamie, it's Elaine."

Shoot.

"Can you please call me back? I'm wondering if you've heard from Derek. Thanks."

The message stopped.

I tossed the phone on my nightstand and dressed for bed. Calling her would have to wait. I was too tired to deal with the conversation. I'd had all the lies I could handle for one evening.

* * *

Maya placed a bottle of acetaminophen and a small paper cup of water on my desk. "Long night, boss?"

"Something like that." I shook three pills from the bottle and drowned them with a gulp of water.

"Caleigh called. She's coming in a bit late today."

I nodded. "Fine." I could only imagine what Daddy Presley was dragging her to today.

"And the new client, Mrs. Vaughn, is here."

I nodded again and straightened the papers in front of me, closing the Livingston folder and placing it in a drawer for later. "Okay. Show her in, please."

Maya walked out with the bottle and cup. "Ms. Bond will see you now."

I stood as an older woman walked in. She had to be nearing eighty. Please don't tell me her geriatric husband was cheating on her. I wasn't sure if I could handle spying on a man with a walker or pacemaker shagging another women...or anyone.

I leaned over the desk and held out my hand. "Mrs. Vaughn, I am Jamie Bond. Nice to meet you. Please have a seat."

After shaking, she sat down and fidgeted with the hem of her skirt of her Donna Karan suit, making sure it covered her knees. "Thank you for seeing me. You come highly recommended."

I smiled on the inside. That was always great to hear. "How may I help you?"

"It's about my grandson, Michael. He just became engaged to a young woman." She touched the pearls at her throat and glanced behind her to the open door.

Perhaps I should've closed it?

She lowered her voice. "May I be frank with you, dear?"

I lowered mine too. "Of course."

"My sweet, trusting grandson is engaged to a two-timing, gold-digging, hussy."

Oh my. I bit my lip.

She narrowed her eyes. "She says she loves him and wants to start a family with him, but I'm not fooled. She's only after his money. One day he will inherit, well, what some people would consider quite a lot."

I uncapped a pen and took notes.

"He is blind in love," she continued. "He will not see what is so obvious. Everyone can see the truth but him. Even our help! Just the other day, I overheard one of the gardeners telling another, 'He can't see she's with him for his money?' I'm afraid Michael is just too trusting. Always has been."

"Tell me about her. Let's start with her name."

"Ruby St. Martin. She's twenty-four and spends her day working part-time at a clothing store in the mall. Here's her vital information. Birth date, social security number, address." She pulled a folded sheet of rose-scented stationary from her purse and placed it on my desk.

I decided not to ask how she obtained the woman's social. I figured Grandma was a crafty, old woman. I rewrote the information onto my pad then filed the stationary beneath it. I'd add it to the folder later.

"And tell me about Michael. You said he's trusting?"

"Oh, Lord, yes. He's always been gullible, even as a child. His late father, my son, would tell me how the neighborhood boys would pull pranks on Michael. They'd tell him how a particular girl liked him, and Michael would approach the girl. Of course she hadn't a clue what he was talking about, and she'd tell him to leave her alone, crushing his tender heart."

"And he never wised up?" I asked wondering how many times someone can mess with a person before that person caught on. Like me with Aiden.

She shook her head. "That is my point. It's so dreadful the way he never learned, never became a bit more…"

"Jaded?"

She pursed her lips. "Exactly. One needs a modicum of cynicism to survive in this world, no?"

"Yes." I jotted down the words: trusting, gullible, and innocent.

"The wedding is scheduled for next month," Mrs. Vaughn said. "I need proof that she's using him before then. I need to prove to Michael that she's a tramp. If I can't, then I'm cutting him off financially."

I looked up from my scribbling.

"I know. I do not want to do it. I love my grandson, but I will not have that woman squander what my late husband worked so hard to build." Her voice came out through gritted teeth.

This woman had spunk and determination, and I admired that, but couldn't she be wrong? What if Michael and Ruby were simply a happy couple? They did still exist in the world. At least before the actual wedding.

"Why do you think she's a gold-digger? Can't Ruby just be in love with Michael?" I asked.

She raised her eyebrows and looked as if I'd asked if money grew on trees. "She is young, hot, and hangs around musicians at nightclubs every night of the week. *Every* single one. My grandson is a portly accountant."

"Oh, I see."

Grandma may be right.

CHAPTER THIRTEEN

———

Caleigh finally crawled in just before lunch. I was at Maya's desk, going through the mail.

"I'm so sorry I'm later than planned," she said, breathless. "After I called in, I kinda fell back to sleep."

"Late night?" I asked. Falling asleep on the job was very unlike Caleigh. Lately, with her dad here though, she was taking more personal time. I didn't mind, as long as it didn't become a habit.

A smile took over her face. "Incredibly. Curtis and I went to this awesome club on Sunset where a friend of his was playing. We had a fantastic time."

"You really like him," Maya said, grinning as she watched Caleigh's face.

"I think he may be the one." She sighed, and I could almost see little cartoon hearts fluttering around her.

"Speaking of the 'one,'" I cut in, "where are we with Stuart Livingston?"

She blew a raspberry. "Nowhere. He's as faithful as they come."

Great. Now I'd have to break the news to his wife. I sighed. "Maya, can you please set up an appointment with Mrs. Livingston?"

"Right away, boss."

I hated upsetting the wives.

* * *

My lunch became tuna on whole wheat with a side salad and a bottle of water in my car, in front of the DA's office. What could I say? I was a sucker for punishment. But instead of only relying on my binoculars, I turned on the walkie-talkie thing I'd snatched from Danny and tuned in.

Aiden's voice immediately filled my car. "I'm waiting to hear from the defense attorney about the plea bargain."

"The Nelson case goes to trial next week. Do you think they'll even consider a plea?" asked another male. He wore a wrinkled, navy suit and needed a comb. His brown hair stuck up in one section at the back of his head. It looked like he took a nap on his desk and forgot to check himself.

Aiden, looking ever so sexy in a gray suit, leaned on the edge of his desk, facing his co-worker. "I think so. The threat of twenty years in jail can make anyone strike a deal."

Wrinkled Man didn't look convinced though.

Aiden's door opened, and Miranda swayed in. "Hi, boys."

Oh, God. Did she think she was Marilyn Monroe?

Both men stopped their conversation and turned to her. Aiden was more subtle with the way he stared at her, but Wrinkled Man may as well have had his tongue hanging out of his mouth, panting and drooling like a dog.

"So what are we discussing?" She practically purred her words.

Wrinkled Man loosened the knot at his tie. "Um, the Nelson case."

She kept her gaze on Aiden, even while the other guy spoke. "Oh, they'll take the plea bargain."

Aiden grinned. "That is what I said."

She stepped an inch closer to him. "Great minds think alike."

"Well, I should be going," said Wrinkled Man.

Aiden said good-bye and thanked him for his help while Miranda just waved him off. She picked a piece of lint off Aiden's suit lapel. Although if I knew Aiden, there really wasn't any on his jacket to begin with, just an excuse to put her hands on him. How obvious.

But he didn't step away. In fact, he looked to her hand, then to her face, and smiled.

I coughed, gagging a bit on some bread crust. Oh, come on.

"What do you say we get out of here?" she asked, filling up the space between them.

I chuckled. There was no way he'd be seduced by Ms. Obvious.

"What do you have in mind?" His voice was lower than usual.

What? How could he fall for that?

"Well, we could go back to my place." She walked her fingers up his chest, from his navel to his chin.

"How about we start with lunch and take it from there?"

"Purr-fect." She literally purred the first half of her answer. I'd swear she was a cat in her last life. A real bitch. Oh wait, that was a dog, huh?

They walked out of Aiden's office, out of view and out of earshot. Darn. Couldn't they have ordered in? What a waste of a lunch hour. I had to eat in my car, while watching those two practically make out on his desk, and now I got to watch them leave to do God only knew what.

Yes, I knew I was freaking out over a man whom I clearly never knew. I couldn't help it. Not only did I fear I still cared, but I hoped it really wasn't true. Talk about gullible.

The front door opened, and they walked out. As they turned the corner, into the parking lot, he had his hand on her lower back.

My phone rang. I reached for it, without taking my eyes off of Aiden and Miranda. "Hello?"

"James." Derek sounded angry.

Crap. Why hadn't I screened my calls? When was I going to learn?

"Good afternoon to you too," I said while watching Aiden hold open his car door for her. I cringed.

"What have you done?" Derek screamed into my ear.

I sighed and lowered the binoculars. "What are you talking about?"

"Elaine called you last night, and you didn't pick up. So then she called me and left angry messages on my phone."

Oops. I guess I should've seen that one coming, but my world didn't evolve around Elaine and Derek. And I told him that. "I've been busy with work. You know, your old agency. The one you're always hounding me about. I missed one call."

"Well I thought you were taking care of her." His tone was clipped.

"She's not a plant or a pet, Derek."

He sighed heavily. "You said you'd help."

"I am. I had drinks with her the other night. I can't guard her or spend every second making sure she's happy. I am working."

How could he be so upset? Yes, I agreed to cover his lie, but I didn't control Elaine's feelings. If she was furious, it was because she could tell he was lying, even if she didn't admit to it. On some level, she assumed what every other woman assumed when her man wasn't being honest. That he was cheating. I could lie for him over and over, and Elaine would still know deep down that Derek was cheating on her.

"Well you knew you'd be working when you agreed." He wasn't shouting any more but his voice still held a terse edge.

"What is it with men today? They don't cheat when they should, they lie about not dating because of dead wives, and now they want me to lie for them while they go sleep with someone else."

"I'm not sleeping with anyone," he screamed.

I had to pull the phone away from my ear. "Then what are you doing?"

"It's personal!"

The phone clicked. He hung up on me. Again.

*　*　*

When I got back to the office, my phone rang. This time I checked the caller ID before answering. I'd learned my lesson. It was Danny. I had a moment of panic, thinking maybe I forgot another physical therapy appointment before I remembered it was Thursday—Mrs. Rosenbaum's day to pick him up before her quilting club. I stared at his name and number for a couple of seconds then pushed the phone away. I couldn't talk to him just yet.

The truth was, as awkward as dinner with Caleigh and her fake fiancé had been, the moment on his couch the other night had been that times ten. Only in a way that I couldn't stop thinking about it. Wondering what would have happened if I hadn't bolted. Part of me kind of wanted to find out. Which is why I didn't answer. I wasn't sure I trusted that part.

I only had a few minutes before my meeting with the only woman in L.A. who would be upset her husband was faithful. I quickly watched the videos Caleigh and Sam had taken of Stuart, hoping he'd hook up. I wanted to make sure it copied over correctly. Nothing like giving a client a blank tape.

I had done that once, during my first case. The poor wife had been furious. It had been the age old betrayal—a hot, young secretary in a tight skirt and three-inch heels bent over his desk. She'd left here seething and saying she was headed straight to her attorney's office. An hour later she'd returned, yelling about how the CD I'd given her was blank. I'd grabbed the wrong one. I'd never made that mistake again.

Of course with the Livingston case, we had nothing but footage of him having dinner with a female co-worker and her husband, drinks with a couple of male friends, and hours spent on the golf course. That had to be an intriguing stakeout. (Eye roll)

Maya's voice boomed over the intercom. "Boss, Mrs. Livingston is here."

I pulled the thumb drive with the video files on it from my computer. "Send her in please."

Maya showed Mrs. Livingston into my office and offered coffee or tea, but the woman declined. She looked distraught and uptight. Her shoulders were hunched. She gripped her purse causing her knuckles to go white. She knew.

"We questioned the women on the list you gave me, and my associates have been following your husband. He is not cheating on you." I slid the drive toward her.

That information should've been received with cheer, relief, a smile, but instead I got a down-turned mouth.

"We had a deal," she tried to explain. "He's changing the arrangement."

"Sometimes things need to change," I said. I hated the way my brain flitted to Danny. I quickly shook it off. "Look, there are worse things in the world than a husband who loves you."

She blinked, and a pensive look overtook her face. Had she not considered this before? Part of me wanted to pick apart her brain and try to understand why she was so adamant about this arrangement. Was she in love with another man but felt obligated to her husband? Had she felt boredom and created this situation?

But it would be unprofessional to question her motives. Especially since we banked on referrals. And another part of me simply didn't want to know. I didn't want to shatter any disillusions I had about commitment. Despite this business, a piece of me still believed in the fairy-tale. It may have sounded stupid, but I figured with all the marriages I watched and helped to dissolve, I'd learn the secrets to what not to do. So when or if I ever tied the knot, I'd have a leg up on all other brides.

"Thank you very much, Ms. Bond. You've been ever so helpful," Mrs. Livingston said, stood up, and walked out.

I hoped a couple of lawyers wouldn't have to draw up divorce papers, citing faithfulness as the reason for incompatibility.

The intercom clicked on again. "There's someone here to see you," said Maya.

"Who is it?"

But before Maya could answer, Aiden appeared in my doorway.

CHAPTER FOURTEEN

———

Aiden entered my office and kicked the door shut with the back of his heel. A scowl sat on his face. "You have to stop following me," he gritted through his teeth.

How dare he barge in here and demand I do anything. I opened my mouth to defend myself, but I hadn't done anything wrong. At least not that he knew about.

I stood and placed my hands on my hips. I could go into the dumb blonde routine and pretend I didn't have a clue, make him spill what he knew before I did. But from experience, that never played out well with Aiden. So instead, I took the direct approach. It couldn't hurt, right?

"I know you're taking bribes. You are the one fixing cases for the Vega crew."

He stepped forward. The stern line of his mouth softened, but his brows still did this crazy arched thing. "How can you even think that?"

A piece of my stone exterior chipped with the disappointed tone of his voice. "Because I saw you with Rocco yesterday."

He didn't respond immediately. It was as if he waited for me to say more. "That's it? That's your big proof?"

"Isn't that enough? You were both huddled together, whispering." I wasn't exactly sure about the huddled part, but it sounded extra secretive.

He slowly shook his head. "Yes, I was with him, because he's my informant."

What? He—ah. Oh crap.

I opened my mouth but didn't know what to say. I needed a moment to process.

"Your informant?" I finally chocked out.

Aiden stepped closer and took one of my hands in his. He led me around my desk, and we sat in the two chairs, side-by-side. He continued to hold my hand, adding the other one to his grip.

What was he doing? Why was he touching me? I didn't mind, of course, but between everything I overheard and saw this past week and now this, my head was spinning.

He reached out and softly touched my chin with his thumb. "What happened to you?"

The scrape was healing fine, but I hadn't applied as much concealer this morning. It was a bright canary shade of yellow with a purple edge.

"I fell. It's not a big deal." The last thing I wanted was a lecture on going into dangerous situations alone. "Explain what you mean by he's your informant." I wasn't stupid, but I definitely wanted him to spell it all out. Make sure we were on the same page this time.

"When I found you in the building, the other day, I believed you. I knew you wouldn't lie to me that you saw someone enter. I wasn't sure who it was or if there really was something going on in my office, but you did, and I've come to trust your gut."

I pulled my hands free of him. Not because I wanted to, but because I couldn't think straight when he touched me. "Go on." I wanted a full confession before I said another word.

"I pulled some surveillance footage of the DA's office hallways from that night. I pulled up the guy's face and ran him through the system."

I leaned back in my chair and crossed my arms over my chest, feeling a bit smug. "And you discovered it was Rocco Diaz."

The left corner of his mouth lifted in a half-smile. "Yes. You were right. That's what you want to hear, isn't it?"

I made a circle in the air with my finger. "Oh, this is more than satisfactory. Please continue."

He softly chuckled. I loved a man who could admit defeat. "I tracked him down to Ventura's."

I wrinkled my nose. "A charming place, isn't it?" I bet being a man he had more luck than I had.

"Yes, it is. So I made Rocco a deal that if he turned informant, I'd offer him immunity and protection."

"And he agreed?"

"He didn't have much of a choice. The surveillance tape showed him breaking and entering. Not to mention what would be discovered at Ventura's. I may not be a cop, but I know quite a few. He could be doing jail time."

Technically he hadn't broken in since the doors were unlocked, but I didn't bother bringing that up. Then it hit me. The tapes showed Rocco entering the DA's office. That meant...

"Wait. You have surveillance cameras *inside* the office building?"

"Yes. We do." He gave me a meaningful look that said he knew I'd been in the offices. Oops.

Then he added a wink. "And I prefer the lace ones."

My cheeks blazed with heat. He'd gotten views of both my pre-laundry and after-laundry panties? I had hoped he'd see them one day. I just would've preferred it was while I was shimmying out of a skirt or performing a provocative lap dance.

"So what's the plan with Rocco?" I wasn't sure if he'd fill me in, but it was easy to ask. Plus I really wanted to steer the conversation away from my ass since I hadn't gotten to see his yet. It was only fair.

"I'm trying to get him to confess what he knows about the big fish."

Oooh, my straight up tactic had worked better than I anticipated. "Vega."

He nodded. "Yes. And hopefully that'll lead to an even bigger fish. Rocco's contact in the office."

Since I was already ahead, I figured why not go for broke. "Miranda Valens."

The corners of his eyes crinkled. "Yes."

I knew it. I almost jumped up and shouted, "Score!" but I refrained. Just barely. "But you've been flirting with her, and taking her to lunch and dinner."

I hated saying it. It made me sound jealous and insecure, and while I wasn't the latter, I didn't want him to know about the former.

He cocked his head to the side. "How do you know that?"

Obviously he didn't know everything. I needed to be careful. As great as this sharing had been, he didn't need to know all of my tricks. I never knew when one of them would come in handy. And while snooping was one thing, I didn't want to trust he wouldn't get pissed off if he knew about the bug.

"There's a clear shot from the street straight into your office. And then I tailed the two of you to…Franco's."

I watched his face, waiting for some tell-tale sign.

His mouth twitched. "I'm sorry you saw that. The only reason I took her there was because I already had a reservation. I go there every Tuesday night since you and I were there."

"You do? Why?"

"They have great fried calamari."

My stomach sank. "Oh."

"And it reminds me of a beautiful blonde who I don't get to spend enough time with."

Okay, so maybe I was acting like a teenager, but I beamed. A huge smile, where I was certain he could see my molars. I couldn't help it. What woman didn't want to hear something like that? And it suddenly didn't matter than he needed time to grieve his wife. Aiden Prince spent every Tuesday night thinking of me. Yeah, very high schoolish.

"Wow, I take back all of the horrible things I said about you."

"You didn't say any horrible things about me."

"It was all behind your back." I flashed him another brilliant smile.

He chuckled.

I took a deep breath and leaned forward. "So what now?"

He hesitated. Maybe this would be the moment he realized he'd said too much and pulled back. But instead of shutting down, he continued, "I'm working on a plan to get Vega and Miranda on tape together with Rocco's help."

I straightened my back, sitting upright. "How can I help?"

He shook his head. "No. I don't want you involved. It's too dangerous."

Here we go again. Same speak, different caveman.

"Danger is my job. I'm not an amateur. I know what I'm doing. Plus, I'm armed."

"The last time you were around bullets, your father was almost shot and your...*friend* almost died."

I heard the emphasis on the word "friend" but ignored it. There was no place for Danny in this conversation right now.

"My gun wasn't involved in that incident, and I cannot control the craziness of a crazy person."

He stood and paced a small area by the chair. "That's my point. I trust you. It's the crazies in the world that I don't. And whoever is working corruption out of the DA's office isn't sane."

I jumped to my feet, determined to not let this go. I could argue all day if necessary. After sharing a bathroom with other models, I had a master's degree in it.

But before I could defend my stance again, he said, "I also don't want to spook Rocco by bringing in anyone else. Especially *CPS*," he said, doing meaningful air quotes.

Oh, he figured that one out, too, huh? He was starting to know me better than I thought. That made part of me very happy. The other part, however, knew I'd have to vary my sneakiness in the future.

"These are truly bad guys. Stay out of it, Jamie."

Then just as quickly as he appeared, he turned and left my office.

I stood in that spot, replaying everything I'd just learned. The feeling of relief that Aiden truly and officially wore the white hat flooded me. I knew it. Sorta. Thing was, though, Aiden may be *too* good. He had a lot more faith in Rocco than I did. Rocco could just as easily be setting Aiden up to take the fall for Miranda's dealings, or worse yet, to conveniently disappear. After all, Aiden just admitted he was the only one who knew anything about this connection.

There was no way I'd just continue to spy on cheating spouses and let Aiden possibly walk into a trap. No, I needed a plan. One that was foolproof. And if I'd learned anything in my two careers, it was that when working with most men, they enjoyed the simple things in life. Fine women and fine alcohol.

Since getting Rocco drunk would be beyond difficult, I opted for option one.

I pulled up my contacts on my phone and dialed the first one listed.

Nothing like asking for help from a couple of old friends.

"Hello?" said a voice with a distinctive Valley Girl accent.

"Apple? It's Jamie."

CHAPTER FIFTEEN

———

"And how do you plan on doing this?" Maya asked, while I reorganized my purse.

Hey, some tasks couldn't be put off.

"It's simple. I'm going to get Candy and Apple to cozy up to Vega, get him to proposition them." In my early days with the agency, I'd gone undercover at a strip club called the Spotted Pony to bust a cheating husband. While the undercover work wasn't going on my official resume any time soon, I had managed to befriend two of the dancers who worked at the Pony. Candy and Apple were always up for a little side job, and rarely asked too many questions. "The cops," I went on, "will be watching and bust him for solicitation. When they do, he calls his friend in the DA's office for help to get the minor charge dropped. They'll have it on tape that Miranda is helping Vega, and everyone is happy."

I pulled an empty, snack-sized bag of Cheetos from my purse and threw it into my trash.

"And you have the police in your back pocket?" Maya asked.

I smirked. "Not exactly. The *cops* are actually going to be me and Sam. And the charge is bogus. But I'm sure if we play it right, we can get the confession on tape."

That was what I hoped anyway. I didn't know what Vega's type was, but Candy and Apple had the attributes most men admired. Candy was curvy and luscious with double D's, or maybe they were G's, F's. How big did boobs come? Apple, on the other hand, was not as curvy but she had an ample bottom (probably the reason for her name) and was very athletic. Her thighs…well, I'd swear she could use them to crack walnuts. One of the women had to appeal to him.

Reaching the bottom of my bag, I shook out crumbs and salt granules.

"Of course, phase one is getting Candy and Apple to Vega. Unfortunately the only way to him that I know about is through the car shop." I took a deep breath. "I'll have to go back."

"Is that a wise choice? Your face is still a bit yellow around the edges."

"Yeah, I'll be fine." But I wasn't as confident as I let on.

I gathered my things, shoved them back into my purse, and headed toward the front door. Just as I was about to grab the knob, it opened and Elaine walked in.

Crap, this wasn't the time.

I contemplated charging past her, muttering an excuse behind me. But after drinks, I couldn't do that to her. And she didn't look right. Her hair needed a comb. Her eyes were bloodshot from too little sleep or too much crying. Was Derek really worth crying over? She must've really loved him. Poor woman.

She widened her eyes upon seeing me. "Oh thank goodness I caught you, Jamie. I really need to talk to you."

I glanced over my shoulder, looking for a legit way out of this, something more than "I gotta go," but it was just me and her. "I'm on my way out. Can it wait?"

"Oh." Her bottom lip trembled for a second.

Please, dear God, don't cry in front of me.

"I was…I, um…"

My chest tightened. The last thing I wanted to do was to leave a distraught woman quivering in my doorway. Plus, Derek's words repeated in my head. "Take care of her."

I tried not to sigh too loudly. "I have an errand to run. If you want to come along, we can talk in the car."

She gave a half-smile. At least the trembling had stopped.

* * *

As I flew down the highway, Elaine's words flew out of her mouth. It felt like every time I stepped on the accelerator, she spoke faster.

"I'm sure Derek's cheating on me."

"I don't think he'd do that," I said even though I didn't believe a word of it. I didn't want to lie to the woman. I liked her. I could even welcome her as a step-mom some day, although the chances of that happening were slim, I was sure. That's it, I was going to kill that man when he returned, and then I'd have to listen to Elaine cry about him being dead.

"He's not exactly the committing type," she said.

She was right about that.

"I knew this, but still I couldn't help myself. He's so adorable."

Clearly she had Derek confused with some other man? Or maybe she was in need of glasses? Okay, so if I took my daughter-glasses off, I could see how he was attractive to women. Tall, dark hair, a year-round tan from living on a boat. He wasn't young, but he was still in great physical shape—at least on the outside. I wasn't sure if his cardiologist would agree. But I definitely saw how he wooed women into his lair.

"Then before I knew it, I was in too deep. I'm forty-two years old. Too old to have been blindsided."

I glanced at the way she was biting her lower lip. If she didn't stop soon, she'd have no skin left. "You can't plan who you'll fall for. It just happens. And it's always by surprise, especially when it's with someone you don't expect."

She stopped the feeding frenzy and looked my way. "You know this from experience." It wasn't a question.

Was she right? And if so, had I fallen for Aiden? Or Danny? Or both?

I shook them both from my head and concentrated on Elaine and Derek. "I believe this will work out for you. Try not to worry too much. I'm sure it'll be fine."

Even if that meant she'd be single and available to meet someone who didn't have the track record of Don Juan.

She took a deep breath, probably sucking back any unshed tears, and gave a curt smile. "You really think he and I will make it work?"

I nodded, completely unconvinced. "Of course."

I should've been shot down by lightning at that precise moment, and considering I was going to my favorite spot on Earth, I probably would be shot by something very soon.

When I pulled into Ventura's, I left the car running, wanting a fast get-away just in case.

"Why are you stopping here?" she asked.

"Just needing to see a man named Vega." I wasn't sure why I told her that. I guess I figured she didn't need more lies.

Her brows formed a line across her forehead. "Are you sure it's safe?"

"You stay here. I'll just be a minute," I said to Elaine and jumped out of the car, dodging the question. I considered grabbing my gun from the glove compartment and hiding it in the waistband of my skirt, but I didn't want to freak her out. Maybe it was a foolish decision. I'd be ready for them this time, though.

I walked toward the building. Clanking metal sounded deep in the garage. I spotted Snake Man and took a single step deeper.

He was in the shadows but came closer. "You again?"

"Look, I really appreciate the help you tried to give me the other day. Turns out, the noise wasn't my car, just something rattling in the trunk." I laughed, trying to play the dumb blonde routine.

Snake Man smiled, but he didn't join in on the laughter. His buddies came from the back, like rats, and stepped alongside him.

"So I was wondering if you could help a girl out again. I was looking for a buddy of yours who works here. Vega?"

One of them visibly tensed. No one said a word. The air hung with danger. But then they looked to one another and Snake Man said, "Who? Never heard of him."

Yeah, right.

I took a couple of steps back, ready to bolt to my car. "Are you sure, 'cause a friend of mine said he worked here?"

They moved forward as one, stepping into the sunlight. I guess I should've taken some comfort in knowing they weren't vampires.

Suddenly, my passenger door opened and Elaine stepped out of the car. "Jamie?" she asked.

I wanted to turn and tell her to get back in. She may have wished for adventure, but this definitely wasn't the kind she needed. But I was afraid that if I turned, one of them would get the upper hand again. That gun sounded better and better with each second.

Snake Man blinked, focusing behind me. "Lanie?" He walked, practically skipped, to the car.

"Carlos? That you, sugar?" A huge smile broke out onto each of their faces.

What the…?

She ran to him and threw herself into his arms. They hugged and laughed.

Seriously?

I looked to his buddies who seemed just as alarmed and confused as I was.

Elaine turned to me, still with Carlos's arm around her shoulders. "Carlos and I go way back. I used to work the night shift with his mom."

"It's been so long," he said to her. "What, like five years?"

She nodded and said something in rapid Spanish that left the three of them laughing. Then she glanced at me but said to Carlos, "We need to talk to Vega about a business deal. Jamie's dad has a boat and would like to make some extra money doing *night runs*, if you know what I mean."

Damn, she was quick and good. Now I understood even more why she believed Derek was cheating. A person that good at lying could point out other liars.

He kissed the top of her head. "For you, Lanie, anything. He hangs out every night at a club he owns in Hollywood. Agev."

She wrinkled her nose. "Is that French?"

His buddies snickered. Obviously it was an inside joke.

Carlos shook his head. "Nah. It's spelled A-G-E-V." He smiled to his buddies.

Oh, clever.

Elaine glanced to me and gave a knowing smile. It seemed the lightbulb went off for both of us at the same time. Agev was Vega spelled backwards.

She gave Carlos a peck on the cheek and another hug. "Thanks, Carlos. You tell your mom hi, okay? And take care."

He nodded. "Will do." The he glanced to me. His smile faded.

I spun around and jumped back into the car. No need to stand there any longer.

Elaine got into the passenger seat and tugged her seatbelt across from her. "His mom is so sweet. You'd love her."

As I pulled onto the street, I glanced at her. She continued to surprise me. Derek would be a fool to let her go. "I'm seriously impressed with your skills."

She winked. "Hey, it's not just Bonds who can be charming enough to get info."

CHAPTER SIXTEEN

———

Sam, Caleigh, and I stood at opposite ends of Spectrum, a dance spot in West Hollywood, keeping our eyes and spy cams on Ruby St. Martin, the possibly gold-digging fiancée of one Michael Vaughn. She was young, a redhead, and considerably hot. I wasn't sure if it was because we lived in the plastic surgery capital of the world, or what, but I'd met an unusual number of exceedingly beautiful women this week.

Not to say there was any shame in having work done. Ruby certainly had. She reminded me of one of those mid-western girls who arrived in Hollywood to become famous and the first thing they did was invest in silicone. Ruby didn't walk. She bounced. Each step became a game of whether or not she'd pop out of her deep V-neck dress. I kept playing the odds, but so far I was losing. Maybe she taped them in. We models did it all the time on fashion shoots. Some of those bikinis weren't more than baby washcloths with string.

I sipped my Appletini and watched Ruby toss a twenty dollar bill on the bar for what looked like a simple Sex on the Beach. Not that sex on the beach was ever simple. The sand got in crevices and… I seriously needed to take my mind out of the gutter.

"Keep the change," she shouted above the music. It was the second time I'd seen her do it so far tonight.

Must be easy to tip well when it wasn't your money.

The place was packed with bodies. Most of them were on the dance floor gyrating to the live music. The current set was a drummer, and a couple of guitar players who seemed to be Caleigh's type—rough around the edges but still without a record. Usually. A glance to Caleigh revealed she wasn't paying any attention to them though. Maybe she really had found "the one" in Curtis.

Ruby, however, didn't care that she was engaged and sported a rock that seemed to weigh down her hand. She smiled, batted her lashes, and did all she could to get the band members' attention. I expected her panties to make their presence on the stage at any moment.

My phone buzzed. I glanced at the ID. It was Danny. I slipped it back into my pocket. I was on the clock. This wasn't the time. I was also still playing the avoidance game.

Besides, I needed to focus on Ruby. This wasn't exactly the club I wanted to be at tonight. I wanted to visit Agev and put my plan into action, but paying clients came first.

A young man in a cowboy hat asked Ruby to dance. They stepped onto the floor just as a girl seated at the bar shouted, "Get off of me."

A guy in a blue, short-sleeve shirt had his hand on her arm. He was saying something I couldn't hear, but he swayed while he tried to stand still, obviously drunk.

A man to the woman's right stood up and stepped between them. "Why are you touching my girlfriend?" he screamed into the drunk guy's face.

Drunk Dude laughed then spit on the floor as if he'd been chewing tobacco, but it hadn't appeared that he was. Maybe it was some kind of male marking, like a tomcat pissing to mark its territory.

Uh-oh, that was never a good sign. Something was going down. Plus they blocked my view of Ruby.

I lifted my arm and spoke into the mic hidden in my cuff bracelet. "I don't have a visual. Can you still see her?" Someone needed to be recording her with our spy cams at all times. Tonight we each wore cameras hidden in pins on our dresses. Danny used to be a part of these missions, sitting in his van recording it all. Luckily he was a good teacher, 'cause now we were able to do it on our own.

Static chirped in my earpiece, then Caleigh said, "Yeah, she's dancing. We got this."

"Nothing worth seeing, boss," Sam said next.

"Okay, let me know if it starts to get juicy, and I'll find another angle."

"Will do," said Sam.

The boyfriend shoved the drunk guy. I expected him to go down for the count, but he performed this backward bending move straight from *The Matrix* and stayed upright. On the upturn, he clocked the boyfriend straight in the jaw.

A bartender whistled to a security guard near the door and pointed. I didn't know how the big and burly dude heard him, but he said something to a friend, who stayed by the door, and approached.

The boyfriend swung and hit the drunk in the stomach.

He doubled over, and while he wheezed for air, the boyfriend punched him in the ear. Boyfriend pulled his hand back and shook out the pain. It was written all over his face, although he tried to hide it.

I wanted to tell him the nose was a better spot, but this was none of my business.

The girlfriend fished ice out of her drink and laid it on a napkin. It definitely wasn't going to be enough. She tried to give it to her boyfriend, but he waved it off, probably not wanting to loosen his macho appearance by admitting he needed it. But his face looked like a candy cane, splotches of red on his pale complexion.

Just as security got there, the drunk puked on the boyfriend's shoes.

I couldn't help but laugh. Just for a moment. Then I pressed my lips firmly together so no one turned and wondered why the blonde thought it was funny.

Everyone at the bar groaned and moved far from the mess, taking their drinks with them.

I put a hand to my nose, just in case, and took several steps to my right. Eventually, after the couple and the drunk were escorted out and some poor, underpaid employees cleaned up the vomit, I was able to see Ruby again.

She was still dancing with the cowboy, oblivious to the spectacle at the bar. There was a moderate amount of space between the two, and she looked off at the stage. Either she wasn't interested in Cowboy, or Grandma was wrong.

I placed my bet on the former, and this time I had a strong feeling I wouldn't lose.

The night seemed to drag. I nursed the one drink while watching Ruby flirt with every musician who took the stage. Once I think she even leaned in on one of the female singers. If any of them took the bait, I hadn't noticed. This continued for hours. But eventually Ruby called it a night, air kissing her good-byes to the bartenders.

She stepped outside, and we followed.

We watched her get into a Town car that just pulled up by the curb. She had a driver? He must've been a Vaughn employee.

"Now what?" Sam asked. "Should we follow?"

I shook my head. "No, if that's the Vaughn's driver, she has to be going home." Alone.

Well that was a bust. Too bad we couldn't ask her if she planned on doing anything picture-worthy before the night began. I still believed Grandma was right though. We'd just have to get the proof another day.

"Let's call it a night," I said.

Caleigh glanced at her watch. "It's not that late. Do I call up Curtis, or go home to Daddy?" She giggled. "Silly question. 'Night y'all."

We'd driven here separately, so Sam and I watched Caleigh get into her car.

"Heading home, boss, or do you plan on another stakeout?" Sam asked.

"Home," I said. "You?"

"There's a little man waiting for me." She smiled and waved as she climbed into her car.

As I pulled my Roadster onto the street I thought of how I was the only one heading to an empty apartment. For some reason that thought caused my car to make a detour, and I found myself in front of Danny's building. When I reached his door, I didn't hesitate, just knocked, knowing that if I waited, I would totally chicken out.

He opened it with a start. "Hi. I called you. Returning calls in person now?" He smiled.

He was in a pleasant mood. That was good.

I laughed, or tried to. It sounded like a car stalling. "I,uh, came by because I need your help." Which wasn't a total lie. While watching Ruby, I'd had a thought as to how I could perfect my Vega plan.

He stepped back and allowed me entrance. But he didn't step back quite enough. My shoulder and arm brushed against his chest as I walked past him, causing me to second guess this whole trip.

The air in his apartment smelled like last night's leftovers. The only light flashed from the TV, and the sound was very low.

"So what do you need help with?" he asked. He stood just a couple of inches behind me. His breath ruffled my hair, causing goosebumps to break out on my arms.

I turned to face him and took a step back. "I need another bug."

He frowned. "Why?"

I couldn't tell him the truth—that it was for Miranda—because he'd say it was too dangerous, and he'd want to get involved. And because this had to do with Aiden, I didn't want Danny involved. I needed to keep both men as far away from one another as possible, for my own sanity. He waved a hand before my face. "Earth to Jamie."

"Right. It's for a new case. Grandma suspects her grandson's fiancée is a gold digger. We need to get the goods." I hated lying to him, but it was the best choice. And from what I knew, I didn't have a tell for lying.

He nodded, staring into my eyes. He either wanted to say something or waited for me to.

I looked to his TV, trying to decipher what he was watching. It was a sitcom with a dad talking to his teen daughter about her boyfriend. The girl rolled her eyes a lot, while Dad made cheesy jokes.

Danny took the hint and headed to his bedroom. The room where he slept, undressed. The room with the big bed.

Stay focused!

I used the moment to take a deep breath and to try to shake the nervousness from my fingers. Of course it didn't help. When he came back, I still felt like leaping out of my skin.

"Here." He handed me a small device.

"Do I use the same walkie-talkie thing?"

He smirked. "Yeah, the transmitter is the same for both. Where's the other bug?"

Oh, right. "Uh, I used that one on another case. The swingers." He didn't need to know that case had ended.

"How's that one progressing?"

"Not the way the wife wants, which is why I used the bug. Don't worry. You'll get them back."

He scratched the top of his head. "I'm not worried."

"Good." I wanted to bolt right then, but it felt rude. Not that standing there with a huge gust of awkwardness felt better.

"So how's therapy going?" I asked.

"Fine. Shoulder feels much better."

I grinned, genuinely happy to hear it. "That's great."

"Yeah." He eyed me suspiciously.

I desperately searched for something…anything to say. "And Mrs. Rosenbaum, how's she doing? Has she brought you more food?"

"You're acting weird," he said.

"I don't know what you're talking about."

Danny pinned me with a hard look. "Really?"

"Yeah. I'm tired, just came from a follow. It's late. You know. The usual." There went that stupid laugh again. If I was seated, my leg would probably be bouncing.

Then, before I realized what he was doing, Danny leaned forward. He wrapped an arm around my waist and pulled me up against his chest. He lowered his head and his lips crushed mine.

I froze. It was so sudden, so unexpected, so…incredibly hot.

I couldn't help myself. I kissed him back. I'd always imagined Danny was a good kisser, but I never realized how good until just that moment. I melted, felt my knees give out, my body dying to mold to his. When his tongue pushed between my lips, my head swirled. I wasn't thinking, just reacting, and every cell in my body cheered, partied.

His other hand cupped my cheek, pushing my hair aside. He reached to the back of my neck and used both hands to try to pull me closer. There was no more space between us though.

That's when I felt him press against my stomach.

I paused. Oh my God, what was I doing?

Palms flat against his chest, I pushed away.

The kiss broke, and he opened his eyes. He had that dreamy, hungry look again.

I touched my swollen lips with my fingertips and momentarily contemplated ripping off all his clothes.

"What's wrong?" he asked, obviously not delighted with my move.

I shook my head. "Nothing. I gotta go."

Without another word, I bolted from his apartment for the second time this week.

I was terrified what we'd be doing the third time.

CHAPTER SEVENTEEN

———

After a night of tossing and turning, and a couple of cold showers (during which I noticed there were no messages from Danny), I arrived at the office in less than tip-top shape. Luckily Maya had my usual waiting for me. I didn't know how she knew when I'd arrive each day, but the coffee was always piping hot and delicious. I sometimes wondered if she hired a barista to hang out in the storage closet.

She winced at my face. Was it the bloodshot eyes, the mascara I smudged beneath my left eye when I almost stabbed myself with the wand, or had my scrape turned an alien shade of lime green? I didn't ask. I didn't need to feel worse. And she was kind enough to not volunteer the information.

"Caleigh's waiting for you in your office," she said, walking ahead of me.

I followed like a slug and nearly whacked my face into the door. I needed to wake up before I got a black eye and added more discoloration.

Caleigh was seated before my desk, filing her always manicured, never chipped nails. She looked up briefly to smile her good morning, but ended up frowning.

I really needed to take a moment with a mirror, some Visine, and a new application of makeup.

I pulled out my chair and sipped my coffee while sitting down. Trying to multi-task meant knocking the cup against my teeth and burning the tip of my tongue.

Mouth. Tongue. My mind jumped to Danny. A flush began below my waist and traveled upward. I set down the cup, before I caused third degree burns, and fidgeted in my seat.

"You okay, boss?" Caleigh asked, pulling me from my thoughts.

I nodded, giving myself a mental shake. There was work to be done, and I needed to find time to slip the second bug into Miranda's office, as well as the whole Candy, Apple, Vega scenario.

"Yes, sorry. Maya, please run down today's schedule."

She swiped across her tablet. "You have a meeting with Levine today."

I looked up sharply. "What for?" I didn't remember making the appointment. The last time I saw my attorney, was a few months ago when the business wasn't doing well and he wanted me to fire one of my girls. Had that only been during the summer? It seemed so much more time had elapsed since then.

"He called late yesterday and said it wasn't important. He was just checking in or something, and asked if I could find a slot for him. I can change it, if you'd like," Maya said.

I nodded. "Please. Call him back and tell him I'll be in touch soon." If it wasn't important, it could wait, but I was mildly curious as to what he wanted. I made a mental note to call him as soon as the chaos in my life toned down.

Maya continued, "You and Caleigh are tailing Ruby this afternoon, and then you're open until tonight when you and Sam are meeting your contacts on the Vega case."

By contacts, she meant Candy and Apple.

"You should have enough time between the two appointments," she said.

This was one of the drawbacks of tailing someone. It wasn't like we were shrinks (at least not the kind with degrees in psychology) and could schedule our clients every forty-five minutes. We never knew how long it would take, so while my schedule looked pretty empty on paper, I'd probably spend half the day sticking to the seats in my car.

Luckily it was Friday, which meant Mrs. Rosenbaum would be picking Danny up from physical therapy again, and I wouldn't have to be trapped in my car with him, pretending last night hadn't happened. Or worse, reliving it.

"If Ruby doesn't meet up with anyone while we're tailing her," Caleigh said. "Then I can follow up on my own when you're with Sam. I'm not seeing Curtis until late."

The phone rang, and Maya rushed out.

Caleigh set down her nail file and smiled. "I'd like to point out that I'm in on time today, and I still had a rocking night with my beau."

I chuckled. "Noted. What did you and Mr. Romantic do this time?"

"We spent the night staring at the stars. First, he surprised me by taking me to the planetarium. It was amazing. I'd never been."

Neither had I. That sounded like something he really thought about beforehand. "How very Ross Gellar of him."

Her baby blues lit up. "I know, right? Then we drove to the beach and watched more. He knows all the constellations. He's an astronomy buff. It was the best. He has the gentlest hands, and those lips…" She fanned herself with her nail file.

My temperature rose again. I crossed then uncrossed my legs. I couldn't deal with this every time someone mentioned various body parts.

"And how is your father doing?" I asked to change the subject. I'd been doing that a lot lately.

"Fine. He's spending the day at the beach, figuring out how to get a tan." She shook her head. "Don't ask. I'm just glad he's out of my hair for the next eight or so hours."

* * *

When I stepped off the elevator (no stairs this time) on the third floor of the DA offices, it looked totally different than during my late-night visits. It was loud and busy—bodies walking along the corridors, phones ringing, and a middle-aged receptionist at the front desk.

I didn't get the luxury of walking, or crawling, past her and going straight back to the offices.

"Can I help you?" she asked, as soon as I stepped through the double doors.

"Yes, I'm here to see ADA Aiden Prince."

She squinted. "Do you have an appointment?"

"Yes. Jamie Bond." What was the likelihood she knew the day's itinerary for every single lawyer on the floor and that I was lying?

She didn't send me packing or call security though. She picked up the receiver and punched in a couple of numbers. She smiled as we waited, then into the phone, she said, "ADA Prince, your appointment is here. Jamie Bond."

I knew Aiden wouldn't refuse to see me, but I wasn't here to actually see him. I needed to get into Miranda's office. If he came out here to greet me, I was in trouble. How would I scoot past him without making him suspicious?

Luckily, she hung up and said, "He'll be with you in a moment. You can have a seat." She nodded toward a couple of chairs to my right.

"Thank you." I sat in one and realized I had the perfect view down the corridor of their offices. It was empty. All I needed was a way to get down it.

Then, since the stars were aligned for me today, a man came in delivering a huge bouquet of flowers. "These are for Madelyn Shore."

"That's me," the receptionist said with a gasp. As she signed for them, I stood and sprinted down the corridor.

I walked straight past Aiden's office, praying he wouldn't fling open the door as I got to it, and into the next one. No knock, no politeness, I just barged in.

Miranda was seated behind her desk reading from a file. When she saw me, she jumped up.

I would've preferred that she'd been elsewhere, but this was my only chance. I couldn't make surprise visits to the office all week without raising suspicions. And who knew if the building would be unlocked tonight. So I didn't stop walking in until I stood beside her desk.

"Can I help you?" she asked. She looked shocked and confused. If she recognized me from the other night, she didn't show it.

"Oh, I'm sorry. I thought this was Aiden's office. The receptionist said I could come on back. She said the third door on the right."

She rolled back her shoulders, like she was getting ready for a fight. "This is the fourth."

"Silly me," I said, without my usual dumb blonde routine to go with it. No widening of the eyes, no cocking my head or lifting my shoulders, no acting innocent. Instead, we stared one another down.

She definitely remembered me. And while she had no clue why I was really here, I assumed she thought I was staking my claim. In a way, I was.

"Jamie," said Aiden's voice from the hall. He stepped in and walked to my side.

I stood on my tip-toes and kissed him on the cheek, as if it was the most natural thing in the world. Something we did every time we saw one another. "Hi. I must've counted wrong, because this is not your office."

He narrowed his eyes and titled his head to the side. He knew I was up to something, but I doubted he'd call me on it in front of her. "I wasn't expecting you." He glanced to Miranda then added, "So soon."

I smiled. Good boy. "I'm early, yes. I was eager for our lunch."

"I thought we were working through lunch, finishing up the paperwork on the Nelson case. We have court first thing Monday morning. The McDonald case," Miranda said.

Nelson must've accepted the plea bargain.

Since I didn't have time for a pretend lunch anyway, I figured I'd give her this one. Just this one. "Oh, if you're too busy, I understand. We can move it to dinner instead." Well, nothing was completely free.

Aiden scratched his head. The poor guy was definitely clueless, but he played along nicely. "If you don't mind." He gave me that look. The one that said, "What the hell are you up to?"

"Of course not. Dinner's better anyway. It's closer to night." Okay, so all of my comebacks weren't paved in gold. But it was too late to take it back, so I just smiled.

Then I turned to Miranda. "So sorry to bother you."

She nodded curtly.

Aiden grabbed my elbow, ready to lead me out, but I still hadn't accomplished my goal. The bug was in my pocket, and if I could just have five minutes to look for the best place to hide it…

"Before you go, Aiden," Miranda said.

Yes! She was finally being useful.

"Can you look this over quickly?"

He let go of my arm and nodded. "Sure."

Instead of giving him time to walk around her desk to where the file lay, she lifted it and approached him. It gave her the opportunity to have their backs to me, for her to press her side against his, as he read over her cleavage, and for her to get a minute of him alone in front of me.

But what she wasn't aware of, was that also gave me ample time to do the exact thing I came here for. I pulled the device from my pocket and eyed a photo on her desk, a small plant on a side table, and the books on her shelves. None of those areas was the right one. It needed to remain more hidden.

Then I noticed her leather tote bag on the carpet, leaned up against the bottom desk drawer. The front pocket was small enough that nothing of value could fit properly, which probably meant she rarely used it.

I bent over, pretending to scratch the back of my ankle, and slipped the bug inside.

When I stood up, Miranda and Aiden parted.

"Ready?" he said to me.

"Absolutely." I didn't need to give her a triumphant smile as I passed to leave. But I did anyway.

Phase two of my plan was complete.

* * *

I couldn't wait to get through the official work day so I could tune into my private eavesdropping session. In the meantime, Caleigh and I tailed Ruby while she spent the afternoon shopping. First it was Rodeo, where she tried on every cocktail dress the trendy new boutique next to the Armani store possessed. Even from my car parked outside, with my wonderful new binoculars, I could tell the poor saleswoman was irritated.

She did a lot of hand-on-hip standing. But money spoke, and Ruby flashed a lot of it. She ended up buying a royal blue, silk wrap dress that hugged her perfectly.

The saleswoman handed her the credit card receipt with a tight-lipped grin. I'd bet she was glad to see Ruby gone.

"I couldn't deal with fussy customers," Caleigh said beside me.

I scoffed. "Me neither." But in a way, didn't we do the same?

Then it was on to shoes. This went much easier. Ruby found several pairs she loved and couldn't decide between. I was surprised she was choosing and didn't just buy them all. She finally settled on a five-inch pair of black and rhinestone encrusted stilettos with straps that criss-crossed around her ankles and legs, up to the middle of her shins. From our distance, the rhinestones made them look more silver.

After this, she stopped at Chanel and went inside. Unfortunately I had no idea what she was buying there. I couldn't see inside from our angle.

"Want me to run in, see what she's up to?" Caleigh asked.

I wasn't sure. If Ruby spotted Caleigh now, and then again possibly later, we could blow our cover. We were good, but Caleigh was hard not to notice.

Before I had to decide though, Ruby emerged, dressed in her new purchases. She'd gone in to change.

Then we followed her to an outdoor cafe for coffee. It appeared that she was waiting for someone else. The waiter pointed to the empty chair across from the redhead. She said something, and when the waiter walked off, Ruby glanced up and down the street.

"We should get a table beside her," Caleigh said.

I shook my head even though she wasn't looking at me. "It'll be too suspicious if she decides to bolt and we're doing the same alongside."

Stakeouts were easiest when you didn't know where your subject was headed. Spy cams and microphones were best when it was an enclosed area, like tailing someone at a party or the other night at the club.

I glanced at my phone to check the time and couldn't help noticing that Danny hadn't tried to call again. Maybe he thought the kiss was a mistake? Maybe he was as glad as I was that we were not talking about it.

A buzz sounded, and I jerked the phone from my purse, but there was no message, no text. I looked over to Caleigh.

She pouted at her phone.

"Is something wrong?" I asked, slipping my cell back into my purse.

"Curtis may not be able to make it tonight. Practice with the band," she said.

"The price you pay for being with a talented musician." I sent her an encouraging smile.

She giggled. "Like a doctor."

In a way, music healed broken hearts, helped people through hard times. Maybe it was better than being a doctor in some ways.

We sat there with our binoculars and watched Ruby sip her coffee and watch for her guest. But he or she never showed. She pulled her phone from her purse and smiled at the caller ID. She spoke to the person (This is where those lip reading skills would've paid off.) then hung up. She slapped a ten dollar bill on the table and jumped up, heading toward the parking garages at the Rodeo Collection.

She wasn't being driven around today. She slipped behind the wheel of a sleek, black Jag and tore out of the lot, heading west on Wilshire.

Following her erratic driving wasn't easy as she connected with the 2, still heading west. Weaving in and out of traffic was a surefire way to either get yelled at or pulled over. She was a menace to other drivers, but I did my best to keep up and not cause an accident as she merged onto the 405 south.

"She's crazy," Caleigh shouted while clutching her door.

I would've replied, but I was too busy silently praying.

Ruby exited the freeway in a decidedly lower rent district than the one she'd shopped in all morning, and after a few blocks pulled into a motel parking lot. It was a two-story motor inn style place with a couple dozen rooms, peeling paint from over-exposure to the harsh California sunshine, and the kind of classy appearance that spoke of rooms by the hour.

"Gotcha," Caleigh shouted.

I slowed down and parked right beside her car.

She went into room fourteen. We'd give her a few, let her settle down, get undressed, get in bed, and then we'd make our move.

"She doesn't seem like the kind of girl who needs a lot of foreplay," Caleigh remarked, clearly getting antsy in her seat.

I smirked. She was right. But I still wanted photos of Ruby and her secret lover in the throes, nothing less. "Give it a bit."

After a few minutes, I spied a housekeeping cart, slowly moving along the second floor, a few rooms down from fourteen. I nodded to Caleigh. "There's our ticket in."

I jumped out of the car, clicking the door shut softly with my hip, and making sure my camera was powered on.

Caleigh approached the housekeeper with a story about how we'd locked ourselves out of our room—silly us. It was clear the women didn't speak much English, but with a few hand gestures, she got the idea and moved to open room fourteen for us. She slowly inserted the key and turned the lock.

I wedged myself in the doorframe so that when she pushed it open, I'd be in direct sight of the bed.

The housekeeper turned, pushed, and stepped back to her cart. If she wondered why the crazy blondes wanted to take pictures of their room, she didn't say anything. I had the feeling this was the kind of hotel were she'd seen stranger things.

The couple hadn't heard us enter the room. Music from an iPod played, and a couple of open beer bottles stood on a night stand next to the bed. The TV was on, even though it was muted. It added light to the room though. Ruby was on top of someone with muscular arms, someone other than her fiancé. Her head was thrown back, hair spilled down to her waist, and she rode him with the wild abandon of a drunk novice on a mechanical bull at a rodeo bar.

I stepped into the room, snapping like mad.

"What the hell—" Ruby started, turning toward Caleigh and me in the doorway. Which was perfect, since I got a clear shot of her face. No way that poor gullible Michael could deny this was his fiancée now.

Caleigh gasped beside me.

And it as I turned my camera to get a couple of shots of the guy, and understood why.

Ruby St. Martin's bull was Caleigh's Curtis.

CHAPTER EIGHTEEN

———

I lowered the camera and stepped back, way back, to the door, trying to somehow shield Caleigh.

Curtis looked up, saw Caleigh, and mumbled, "Oh shit."

"You sonofa—" Caleigh was too much of a lady to finish that. Instead, she shot forward, grabbed the two open beer bottles from the nightstand, and poured them on the couple, making sure to direct the stream over each of their heads. The liquid dribbled down the middle of their faces with perfect precision.

Ruby leapt off Curtis (Boy, that had to hurt.) and fell onto the other side of the bed, sputtering. She blinked and screamed and then blinked and screamed some more.

"What the hell are you doing?" Caleigh screamed louder.

I was pretty sure it was a rhetorical question.

"How could you?" She threw the bottles at the wall, past the bed.

They hit but didn't break and fell to the carpet with a thunk.

Their non-destruction just seemed to anger Caleigh more. She reached for the lamp, but it was bolted down.

Curtis tried pushing Ruby off the bed, so he could get up. "Look, I can explain."

Seriously, dude?

"Ohmigod, my extensions," Ruby sputtered, smacking Curtis as if it was his fault she was covered in beer.

"Caleigh, please," Curtis said, ignoring the screaming redhead.

"You lying sack of—" Caleigh found his clothes by the foot of the bed and threw them out the door, into the parking lot.

Then she pushed past me back into the room, looking for more ways to hurt him.

Luckily the heavy stuff wasn't budging. Thank goodness for cheap motel security.

"All those nights. You told me you could fall for me, that I was the best thing that ever entered your life," Caleigh fumed.

Ruby stood up and turned on Curtis. Her bare breasts bounced. "You told me the same thing."

Both women did this guttural scream-slash-moan sound. I took a step closer to the door in case I needed to run for it.

Caleigh jerked open the nightstand drawer and found something that wasn't bolted down. She picked up a book and held it over her head, ready to throw it at him.

Ruby screamed, "Not the Lord."

Caleigh looked up, realized she held the *Bible*, and put it back in the drawer. She reached for a pillow and began beating Curtis, who was still stuck on the bed, between both women.

At first I just stood there. I was in shock and felt raw seeing Caleigh so upset. But then the pillow started slipping from its case, and soon Caleigh was hitting him with her own hands.

He tried to block his face and head with his arms. At one point his mouth set into a grim line, and I worried he'd eventually strike back.

I slung the camera's strap over my head and lunged forward. I grabbed Caleigh beneath her arms and tried to pull her backward. She dug her heels into the carpet and fought me at first, trying to twist out of my hold.

"Caleigh, come on. We have to go." Even though this seemed like the sort of "what happens in the ghetto stays in the ghetto" type of motel, eventually someone was likely to call the cops on two screaming women. I didn't want to be held for questioning. I didn't want Ruby to find out we were here because of Grandma Vaughn until she decided to show the evidence to Michael. And boy, was there plenty of it.

A foot from the door, I spun Caleigh around and blocked her way before she had time to start beating Curtis again. I stared into her eyes.

They were wild, and she didn't seem to see me.

"Let's go," I said in my loud and stern voice.

She blinked, sent one last icy gaze Curtis's way, and stomped to my car.

I glanced back at the room.

Ruby had run into the bathroom. Curtis sat on the edge of the bed, facing the wall, his back to me. He must've felt my staring because he turned his head and glanced at me.

Anger bubbled up inside my chest. I desperately wanted to hurt him for Caleigh, but if I didn't leave right away, she'd come back in. And if I didn't get her out of there, I risked her doing something she couldn't take back.

Once we were strapped in my car and on the highway headed back to the office, the sobbing began.

I handed Caleigh a small pack of tissues from my purse, while keeping my eye on the jerk driver ahead of me. He or she kept swerving in and out of my lane.

I didn't know what to do about Caleigh. I couldn't leave her alone, but I didn't have much time before Sam and I were to meet Candy and Apple at Agev. I hated that I couldn't spend the evening getting drunk with my friend. Then I remembered Maya was still at the office, so I pulled out my phone and called.

"Bond Agency."

"Hey, it's me. Do you have plans tonight or can you stay a bit late?"

"As long as you need." Maya sounded worried. She could probably hear the tension in my voice. "What's up?"

"I'm almost there. I'll explain then. Just…" I glanced at Caleigh, who was slumped in the seat, her head pressed against the window. "Get some margaritas ready."

* * *

When we pulled in, I parked right in front of the door and helped Caleigh inside.

Maya and Sam were standing in the doorway waiting, a drink in each of their hands. They both looked at Caleigh's wet, mascara caked up face and then to me. Deep questioning frowns creased their foreheads.

"We found Ruby in bed with…" I nodded toward Caleigh.

Sam's eyes doubled in size. "Curtis?"

"Don't say his name," Caleigh said through gritted teeth. She grabbed the drink in Maya's hand and downed it.

We stepped into the lobby, and I spotted Danny. Crap. What the heck was he doing here? I turned to Sam, grabbed that drink, and repeated Caleigh's actions.

He stepped forward. "Hey, I thought we could chat, but I guess this isn't a good time."

I shook my head sharply. "No. Definitely not."

At least now I knew why he hadn't called. He wanted to do a blitz attack.

"How'd you get here?" I asked, a bit annoyed that I had to deal with this right now.

"Mrs. Rosenbaum."

I should've known. This meant he'd need one of us to give him a ride home. I'm sure he planned on it being me, but those plans would have to change. I glanced at the time. Sam and I had to leave very soon.

Maya poured another round of drinks for Caleigh and me. I declined, and Caleigh took both. She collapsed into a chair. "I can't believe the bastard is a cheating…"

Maya and Sam surrounded her. One patted her arm, the other rubbed her back.

"Dog?" Maya offered.

"Asshole?" Sam asked.

Caleigh nodded. "Both." She took a deep, cleansing breath and sipped one of the margaritas.

I glanced at Danny, who was watching my friends. I think he knew the last thing Caleigh would want right now was a man's opinion.

"I don't understand how I could've been so stupid," she said between sobs. "I thought he loved me, and this whole time he's been cheating on me."

"What?" shouted a deep voice by the door. "I'll kill him."

We all looked over, and Mr. Presley stood there. His hard, cold stare zeroed in on Danny.

Oh crap. We were definitely going to be late.

Mr. Presley took five giant steps toward Danny, his arms extended like Frankenstein, as if he planned on strangling Danny to death.

Danny's eyes darted back and forth, searching for a place to hide. "Mr. Presley, I can explain."

Probably not the best thing to say. It made him sound guilty.

For an older man, Mr. Presley had a lot of power in his steps. He chased Danny around the lobby, one fist in the air, ready to slug him.

"Caleigh, tell your father the truth," Danny shouted. "I don't want to hit him, but I will defend myself."

Mr. Presley cornered Danny by Maya's desk.

Caleigh jumped up and stepped between them. "No, Daddy, it wasn't him."

"You just said he cheated on you." Mr. Presley's chest rose and fell rapidly.

She squeezed her eyes shut. Tears fell from the corners. "It wasn't Danny. It was another man."

He lowered his arm. "You mean, you've been cheating on your fiancé?" His voice was hushed, as if he hadn't wanted anyone else to hear.

"No, Daddy. I've been lying to you."

And that was our cue. I looked to Sam and nodded toward the door. It was time to make our escape. Plus, I didn't want to see Mr. Presley's head explode.

* * *

On the way to Agev, I got a call from Elaine. She insisted on not missing the fun. I thought about arguing, but I figured if I took her with me I killed two birds with one stone— happy Elaine, no angry calls from Derek. Besides, she had been the one to get the info on where to find Vega. Without her, I don't know what I would've done. So we swung by her place to pick her up and used her bathroom to change into our cop outfits Sam had rented. But as we all piled back into my car, I made sure she understood that she was not to leave the car, under no circumstances. Derek told me to take care of her, not risk her life.

She nodded with a big smile, eager for the adventure.

Then we met up with Candy and Apple across the street from the club and wired them with the bracelet mics and brooch spy cams we used for surveillance. We watched them walk across the street and inside.

I turned on the transmitter and cradled my laptop between the front seats, cuing up the recording program connected to the girls' mics and cameras. The camera angles came up on a split screen, so we could watch both at the same time. Danny had trained us well.

Whatever we caught on video tonight couldn't be used legally, but I wanted all of our bases covered just in case something could be used later on. And in case it got ugly once Sam and I went inside.

Candy and Apple went to the bar and chatted and flirted their way around the room. It took a while, but eventually they caught Vega's attention and were invited into the V.I.P. area.

Vega was a short, stocky man with a high-pitched, girly voice. I'd bet he had a huge Napoleon complex. But he dressed well in a sharp, black suit with a white shirt and a silver tie. He had a clean-shaven head that reminded me a bit of Pitbull, the singer. But where Pitbull had a sexy demeanor, Vega was all brute.

"Are the two of you one treat, like a candy apple?" One of his two thugs asked. The other laughed. They both towered over their boss.

I rolled my eyes, but I guessed the girls were used to those types of comments, especially working at The Spotted Pony. They obviously didn't mind because they giggled along.

For the first twenty minutes, the girls and men chatted about the club, drinks, and dancing. Then Apple performed a mini lap dance for one of the thugs. All the men cheered. Of course.

The girls flirted their pants off, almost literally, but it didn't seem to be going anywhere. I started getting impatient. I wanted to get out of the car and pace, but I didn't want to miss anything. This had to work. If not, I didn't know how else to get the goods on Hot Lips Miranda.

"So how about you and we go someplace more private?" Candy said. She sat on one of Vega's thick, squat thighs, while Apple was on the other.

"Both of you?" He looked from one to the other, and surprisingly, he kept his gaze on their faces.

"We do everything together." Candy giggled.

"And what do you have in mind?" And there were the boob gazes. At least I knew he was straight.

"Anything you can afford." Apple sounded sultry.

"Oh, I have plenty of money, girls. And I can go all night," Vega finally said.

The thugs nodded and chuckled like a couple of school girls. I'd never understand some men when it came to their sexual prowess.

"Us too," Candy and Apple said in unison.

I turned to Sam. This was it. I hoped. I held my breath, waiting for his response.

"Then we need to get out of here," he said.

And there it was. It may not have held up in real court, but it was perfect for Bond justice.

Sam and I flung open our doors and stepped out of the car. Glock on my hip, I turned to Elaine and said, "Stay put."

She nodded, pulling the laptop onto the backseat beside her.

Then I paused. "If by some chance this doesn't go down as planned... if it looks like we're in trouble...call the cops."

Elaine looked up, wide-eyed.

I smiled. "Don't worry. It'll be fine." At least I hoped so.

I turned and marched across the street with Sam. We headed inside and past the front security who paid us no attention. They were too busy breaking up a couple of girls slapping one another. There was nothing like alcohol to bring out the cage fighter in people.

We rounded the corner to the V.I.P. Section. No one tried to stop us, but several people turned and whispered. Despite our good luck so far, I began to sweat. Nerves jumbled in my stomach so bad, I winced a couple of times.

Candy and Apple were still on Vega's lap. The thugs were taller and much scarier looking in person.

"Eduardo Vega, you're under arrest for solicitation." I deepened my voice and hoped it gave me an edge. I feared spewing my lunch all over the floor, like that drunk last night.

Candy and Apple jumped up, scooting to the side. I hoped their cameras still caught the footage. I'd instructed them how to stand once we arrived, but under duress it was easy to forget. I couldn't afford to turn and look.

The bodyguards reached for their guns in their side holsters.

Sam and I withdrew first. "Guns down, boys. Unless you'd like to see the inside of a jail cell too."

They just stood there, hands on the butts of their pieces, contemplating whether or not they'd…what? Pull a gun on a couple of cops? Take the odds of who'd shoot first? This was crazy. Who did they think they were? The fake cop in me grew pissed.

"Officers, what seems to be the problem?" Vega said. "The young ladies and I were just talking."

He didn't seem at all bothered about being arrested. I was sure, at some point in his life, this was a common occurrence.

"Actually, they propositioned you and you agreed. We have it on tape." I didn't mention Candy and Apple. I didn't want to risk them getting hurt. I snuck a glanced their way this time and saw that, just like we'd planned, they both pulled shocked faces. Good girls.

The thugs didn't move, and by the look of their weapons, I was certain that if they shot, Sam and I wouldn't make it to the hospital.

"You need to put your hands on the back of your heads," Sam said to the thugs. When they didn't listen, Sam focused her gun on Vega.

"I'd listen to her if I were you. My partner has perfect aim," I said.

"A police officer won't shoot a civilian," Vega said. But I saw the moisture on his upper lip. He was as worried as I was.

I thought of Elaine. I prayed she wasn't calling 911. But considering how my shirt was pressed to my back, I knew this charade had gone on long enough.

I lowered my gun, but Sam held hers steady. "Mr. Vega, we won't be hauling you into the station right now, but you better call your lawyer, because we're returning with a warrant. And my partner and I will be more than happy to tear this place apart."

We backed out of the roped-off section. When we reached the corner, Candy and Apple ran out the front. Sam and I took our time, careful Vega and his thugs didn't follow.

Once outside, adrenaline kicked in big time, and I ran across the street to my car. Inside, I let out a deep, shaky breath and yanked off the cop hat.

"Oh my goodness, that was crazy," Elaine said.

If Vega or the thugs came outside, I didn't want them to recognize us. What cops drive a cherry red convertible? I shrugged out of the shirt, grateful I'd worn a white tank beneath.

Candy and Apple waved as they sped away in their car. While they smiled, they also looked a little less tanned than usual. Were they ready to toss their cookies too? Would they volunteer so easily to help me out next time?

"Did it record it all?" I asked Elaine. "Did the girls capture enough of it after Sam and I arrived?"

Elaine shut the laptop. "Yes, I saw the whole thing. I couldn't make out your and Sam's faces, though."

Just as well, in case I needed to show this to Aiden.

I turned on the car and kept my eye on the rearview mirror as I drove off. Then I said a silent prayer that Vega really did call his lawyer. Miranda.

CHAPTER NINETEEN

————

I dropped Sam off at the agency to get her car. The office was empty, which meant Caleigh, Mr. Presley, Maya, and Danny had left. Good. I didn't have time to deal with anything else. I had a bug to listen to.

"Thanks for tonight, Sam. And give Julio a hug from me."

"Will do. If you need anything else tonight, like tailing…" She was referring to Aiden. "Just give me a call."

I appreciated it. I glanced at Elaine and needed a different kind of favor. "Do you mind dropping Elaine off? I need to get on something." If I got stuck alone with Elaine in the car, there was a good chance she'd want to talk about Derek. I didn't have time or patience for that.

"That's fine."

"I had a great time, Jamie. Thanks for letting me tail along." Elaine climbed out of my car.

"You're welcome." I didn't think Derek would be happy I took his possible girlfriend, possible ex, on a dangerous stakeout, but he usually had no room to talk. He definitely wasn't the pillar of safe or moral behavior.

They both got into Sam's car. I watched them pull out of the parking lot before taking the transmitter from my purse and switching it on. Voices and laughter filled my car at a deafening roar. I lowered the volume and listened closely. Had I missed the call? Damn, I hoped not.

Then a baby cried and a voice said, "With Pampers, your baby will sleep through the night."

It was the television. Fairly certain I hadn't missed anything juicy, I drove to my apartment.

When I got upstairs, I kicked off my shoes and continued listening to Miranda's choice of TV shows. I changed out of the rest of the uniform and made a mental note to give it back to Sam so she could return it. The scene with Vega had gone better than I'd anticipated. Having Sam as my partner definitely gave me more confidence. If either of the thugs had taken a shot, I knew Sam would've put a bullet in Vega's skull. Of course, it wouldn't have mattered if I'd been dead.

I set up the transmitter on the coffee table, beside a portable tape recorder. It was old, but it still worked. Derek always said, get proof of everything. Copy copies, just to be safe.

As I heated up three day old chicken stir-fry from the Chinese place around the corner, Miranda flipped channels. A soda can popped, and I heard slurping. Too bad I couldn't publicly post her unladylike slurps somewhere.

A microwave dinged in the distance, and I heard scrambling then heels on a hardwood floor.

My microwave dinged too, and I took my dinner out, bringing it with me to the couch. I turned on my TV and muted it; then I flipped channels until I found the one that matched the sounds from her set. She was watching a rerun of *Modern Family* on cable. Interesting. I pegged her more as a crime drama kinda girl, with a penchant for villains.

Soon her slurping was accompanied by chewing. I listened closely, having fun deciphering the sounds. The crunch wasn't crisp enough to be potato chips or pretzels. And since I'd heard the microwave, it had to be popcorn.

She got up again, and a few minutes later I heard a toilet flush in the distance. Just what I wanted to hear. At least she hadn't taken her purse into the bathroom with her.

I contemplated pouring myself a glass of wine, but I was exhausted and didn't want to fall asleep on my spying.

The episode ended, and another had just begun when her phone rang.

I flinched, nearly dropping my fork. Her purse must've been right next to it.

I brought the transmitter to my ear, and held the recorder next to it, not wanting to miss a syllable. It had to be Vega.

"Aiden, hi, babe," she said.

My gut tightened. Why the heck was he calling now?

"No, I haven't eaten. I'd love dinner."

I rolled my eyes. Hadn't she just stuffed her face with a bag of popcorn?

"That's sounds great." She did that purring thing.

I wondered which restaurant they would end up at. If he took her to Franco's, I'd scream.

"No, I'd love to come over. Give me a few? Okay, see you soon."

What? Was he serious? I held the transmitter so tight, a cramp formed in my hand. I loosened my grip and reminded myself it was only an act on his part. He just needed to get closer to her to get at the truth. Besides, what did I care? I wasn't dating him.

I set everything back on the coffee table and checked my phone for messages from Danny. None. Not that I was dating him either. I contemplated calling him, but I didn't know what to say. I didn't want to talk about the kiss, but I didn't want to *not* talk about it either. Just like I didn't want to repeat it but, oh man, did I. Clearly I didn't know what I wanted. And I also had Aiden. Sorta.

Miranda's phone rang again.

I held my breath. Could it now be Vega or was Aiden calling back, asking her to bring the whipped cream?

"Hello? Wait, what? Slow down Eduardo."

Bingo!

I jumped, hitting my knee into my plate. Dishes rattled against my glass coffee table top.

"Ssshh," I whispered.

"Yes, I'm well aware my job is to keep the cops away from you. That's what I've been doing. Maybe you should try keeping it in your pants," Miranda said.

I chuckled. I had to give her a point for that one.

"Look, I'll take care of it. In the meantime, relax. Besides, there's something more important. I spoke with Rocco. He says Prince is trying to make him turn state's evidence."

Shit. I knew Aiden couldn't trust Rocco.

Panic seized my gut. How long had Miranda known? I had to call him, warn him before she went over to his place…

"Don't worry about it. I'm on my way over right now. I will clean up this mess for good."

Oh my God. She was going to kill Aiden!

CHAPTER TWENTY

———

I dialed Aiden's number, and it went straight to voicemail. I ground my teeth. Now was so not the time for him to screen my calls. I didn't bother leaving a message. By time he got it, Miranda might have already killed him.

Wouldn't you know it, my phone picked that moment to ring, Danny's number flashing. I ignored it, shoving it into my pocket.

I grabbed my shoes, keys, transmitter, and Glock and ran out the door. I winced as my soft, recently slathered with an aloe and lavender moisturizer feet landed on pebbles on the race to my car. Once behind the wheel, I slipped on my shoes and shoved the key into the ignition. I pressed on the accelerator too hard and made the car roar to life. I tore out of my parking garage and down the street.

Up ahead was a red light, and if it hadn't been for the serious looking middle-aged man in the car next to me, I would've considered driving through it. I tapped an erratic beat on the steering wheel.

"Come on, come on, turn."

Sounds from the transmitter told me Miranda had left her place and had just started her car. I may have had a lead, but I knew she lived closer to Aiden.

The light changed, and I flew ahead. The middle-aged man laid on his horn, probably shouting obscenities and taking down my plate number. If the police wanted to follow me to Aiden's, they were welcomed to.

Sounds of loud bass came from the transmitter and then quickly faded away.

I turned into the next lane, swerving around a snail's pace older couple. Some people shouldn't be allowed to drive past dark.

My heartbeat boomed in my chest. I had to make it in time.

I was only about five blocks away when Miranda's engine stopped. Unless her car mysteriously stalled or the engine fell out, she'd gotten to Aiden's.

"No, no, no," I chanted, taking a turn so fast I might have tipped on two wheels.

Miranda knocked on his door, then said, "Hi," in that nauseatingly seductive way of hers.

"Hello, come on in. I'm surprised you came this way…"
Static interrupted his words. What was he talking about?

I punched my dashboard and drove faster, almost killing a stealthy garbage can.

Her heels clicked on his floor and a door shut. Soft jazz music played in the background. Was that his seductive gameplay? What, was he thinking he'd get a confession over pillow talk?

Seriously, Jamie. Now was not the time for jealousy.
"Dinner's almost ready," he said.

I jerked my steering wheel, making a wide right turn. His house was up ahead.

"I don't think that'll be necessary," she said, but her voice had changed. Instead of the sex kitten act, her tone was hard and flat.

Oh God.

I stopped outside his house, threw the car into park, and raced up his walkway, not bothering to shut my door. A robbery was the least of my worries. I prayed Aiden's front door wasn't locked. I'd throw myself through a window if I had to.

I'd left the transmitter in the car. I had no idea what was going on. The only thing on me was my gun, and I planned to use it if I had to.

I twisted the doorknob. It didn't budge. What the…

The drapes weren't drawn, but I could barely see inside. It was dim, almost dark. A light came from somewhere in the house though. Were they already making out on the sofa, or God forbid, his bedroom? No, he wouldn't allow it to go so far. Plus, she had sounded done with playing games.

I walked around the house, my ears straining for any sound, eyes staring into every window I found. I got closer to the light source and realized the living room was carpeted. When Miranda arrived, her shoes hit hardwood or…tile.

The kitchen.

I ran to the back of the house and sure enough, a light shown bright beneath a back door. I grabbed the doorknob and yanked. It turned all the way. Then I threw open the door just as I saw Miranda pull a gun out of her tote bag.

I ran forward and flung myself on her back, wrapping my arms and legs around her neck and waist. She cried out and the gun clanked to the floor. Mine was in the back of my waistband. I couldn't hold on and reach for it at the same time.

"Aiden, get the gun," I screamed.

Miranda walked backwards, bumping into a chair and slamming us into a wall.

My head whacked against the edge of a picture frame. The air got knocked out of me, and I groaned, my grip on her loosening. I slipped off her back onto my feet, but I wobbled, unsteady, and unfocused.

For some reason, instead of turning and strangling, or punching, or whatevering me, she ran to the counter.

I took a deep breath, or tried to, and managed to focus on Aiden.

He walked toward me. "Are you alright?"

Something glinted in his hand. Was he holding the gun?

"I'm fine," I said.

He started to walk out of the room. "I'm calling the cops."

"I wouldn't do that if I were you," Miranda said.

My hand went for my weapon, but before I could do more than graze it with my fingertips, she wrapped an arm around my throat from behind. And I realized what she'd gone for on the counter. She held a chef's knife at my throat.

"Well, what do we have here?" she asked, and yanked my gun loose.

Well this wasn't how I thought this evening would pan out.

"Hmm, which should I use?" she asked. A rhetorical question as she threw my gun across the room. It hit the floor and slid under Aiden's stove. Of course.

"I think I prefer this one." She pressed the blade against my throat. "It's quieter, won't alert the neighbors. Plus there's an added bonus of watching all the blood drain from your lifeless body."

I figured that wasn't the time to point out that a bullet hole would have the same result.

"Miranda, let her go," Aiden shouted. He held Miranda's gun up, had aimed it at us.

I prayed that he didn't let it go off. I doubted he had the same great aim as Sam.

He walked around us, until he stood squarely in the kitchen, between us and the back door. Smart move, but that didn't mean she wouldn't find another way out.

She backed us out of the kitchen and into a dim hallway. I couldn't tell where it led, but I assumed we'd be in the living room and out the front door soon. Unless one of us stopped her first.

"Miranda, this is insane. You can't get away with this," Aiden said, following us into the hall.

She laughed in a cackling witch kind of way. "You think so? You've been seriously underestimating me since we started working together, Aiden. Is it because I'm a woman, an attractive woman?"

Another step and my hip bumped into a side table. The lamp swayed back and forth but stayed upright.

"No, that's not it," she said, answering her own question. "Your fair-haired darling here is female, and you believe she's capable. Or do you? Does he think you're an idiot too, sweetheart?" she whispered in my ear.

A shudder ran down my back. Then my phone rang from my pocket. I flinched. I'd forgotten it was in there.

It must have caught her off guard too because her hold on me loosened.

That was my chance. I raised my arm and jabbed my elbow into her boob. Now, I knew that had to hurt.

She moaned and not in a good way.

Then I sank my teeth into the fleshy part of her hand and chomped down.

She screamed and opened her hand. The knife fell to the carpet.

I lunged forward, out of her grasp, and fell to my hands and knees.

"Miranda, don't," Aiden shouted, taking a step forward.

I looked back and saw Miranda bend down and grab the knife again. She reached over her head and aimed it at me. Then she lunged.

Before I could scramble out of the way, a shot rang out.

Miranda doubled over and fell to the floor.

I looked back at Aiden.

He stood in the middle of his living room, gun shaking in his hands.

CHAPTER TWENTY-ONE

———

I paced my silent office back and forth around my desk as the sun rose. I'd spent most of the previous night answering a bajillion questions for the police, giving them my recording of the call between Miranda and Vega, and worrying about Aiden. From the moment he'd shot Miranda's gun until the detectives showed up, he stared off into space. I barely got him to speak, and when I did, all he kept saying was how he was a lawyer, not a killer.

I'd tried to comfort him with a hand on his arm, but he'd pulled away. I knew it was the shock. The first time I shot an actual human being and not a paper silhouette I felt numb for days. And mine didn't result in a death. I hoped things felt different for him in the morning. I wanted to call and talk to him, to know he was okay, and to know he wasn't putting the blame on me...on us.

That thought tugged at my chest. It was the reason for yet another night of tossing and turning. I'd managed a couple hours of sleep before getting up and driving to the agency. I couldn't just sit at home and worry.

I bumped into my desk, which rattled a cup of pens. I grabbed my phone and for the umpteenth time pulled up Aiden's number. I tugged on my top lip with my teeth.

I chickened out though, and instead of calling I texted.

R u free 2nite? Id love 2 decompress over dinner.

Done. I set the phone down and continued pacing.

Suddenly my office door flew open. It smacked against the back wall. In the doorway stood Maya, her legs widespread apart, a look of fear on her face. In her hand was a bottle of pepper spray—her finger on the button, ready to shoot.

I flinched, my heart leaping into my throat. "What are you doing?"

Tension left her body and she let out a sigh. "God you scared me. I thought we had an intruder." She glanced at her hand and lowered her arm.

"I didn't want to sit at home. Didn't you see my car in the parking lot?"

She shook her head. "I had Brandon drop me off. I wasn't exactly looking at anything but his eyes. I didn't think anyone would be here today. Then I heard a noise and…well, you're lucky I didn't reach for my gun first."

"Very sorry to scare you." I fell into one of my chairs, my heart racing.

She took a tentative step forward. "Are you alright?"

I shrugged. "As alright as I can be considering this is my third shooting in the past three months." Perhaps I'd set a world record or something. Was there a category for gun fire in Guinness?

She sat beside me and rubbed my arm. "You should be home resting."

I shook my head. "No, that's the last thing I want. I need to keep busy. Are there any new cases?"

She gave me that look. I hadn't figured out exactly what it meant yet, but it always made me feel like I was a child in need of a hug and a cookie. "No, but you have a couple of appointments on Monday. I can reschedule them."

"Don't you dare. I need the distraction." Especially if Aiden still hadn't called by then. "What are you doing here on a Saturday? Why didn't you stay in bed with Brandon?"

"He had some stuff to do at the office, so I figured I'd come in and get caught up on some paperwork."

I glanced at my desk, wondering how I'd spend the morning. Derek was coming home today. I planned to take him to lunch and make him spill about the bimbo he was cheating with. "Hey, I have a job for you. A quick one, I hope."

"What is it? Should I grab my tablet?"

I smiled. I loved her efficiency. "I think you'll remember this. I need you to find out what's been going on with Derek. He went out of town on some mysterious mission on Monday. He's returning today, but I'd like to know where's he's been."

"You got it. Anything else?"

I backtracked the last twenty-four hours. "Mrs. Vaughn. I need to tell her the good news and give her the tape."

Maya nodded. "I already set up that appointment for Monday morning. She's away this weekend. I guess she didn't think you'd find the dirt so fast. She sounded practically giddy on the phone when I told her you'd like her to come in. I didn't say Ruby was found cheating, but I guess she could tell."

I chuckled. Nothing like a happy client. Poor Michael. And poor Caleigh.

"How's Caleigh dealing?" I asked.

"Not great but telling her father she lied took precedent. He's leaving today too. She plans on spending their last few hours before his flight together."

"How did that go?"

"Surprisingly well. Mr. Presley was more hurt that she lied to him, and felt the need to lie to him, than he was about the actual lie. Turns out he didn't think Danny was a suitable husband for her anyway."

"Ouch. Poor Danny." Though I had to chuckle. I couldn't imagine any father jumping for joy at little-black-book Danny dating his daughter.

Maya nodded. "Mr. Presley said that Danny didn't seem interested in his princess. That he seemed more interested in her boss." There went that look again.

"Me?" I squeaked out, my mind immediately going to the feel of Danny's lips on mine.

Luckily Maya was saved answering that as my phone rang. Danny's number came up. Oh boy. Talk about timing.

I contemplated ignoring it, waiting for my hormones to calm down and the vision of his perfect mouth to dissipate from my thoughts. But I needed to thank him for calling last night and distracting Miranda. I bit my lip, torn.

Maya took her cue to leave. "I'll find out about Derek."

As she shut my door behind her, I gathered up my courage (and hormones) and answered the phone. "Good morning."

"Seriously? That's all I get," Danny shouted in my ear.

I took a deep breath. What had I done now? "So it's not a good morning. What's wrong, sunshine?"

"I have to find out about you almost dying, again, from the *L.A. Times*?"

Oops.

"You're lucky I'm not allowed to drive or I'd be at your place this minute."

He didn't need to know I wasn't at home in bed resting.

"Sorry. It was a long night, and I crashed." Sorta. "I wasn't keeping you in the dark on purpose."

He sighed. "That's not the worse part, James. I could strangle you for pulling this behind my back."

As if I planned on almost being stabbed to death?

"I don't care what my doctor's orders are. No more physical therapy. From now on…starting Monday I am appointing myself your official bodyguard."

Oh boy.

"I'm not allowing you out of my sight, and there will be no arguments about it."

This time I appreciated his desire to protect me, even if it wasn't necessary. "That may be a little awkward while I'm showering."

"I think I can manage," he answered, a whole new tone in his voice. Deep. Sexy. Dangerous.

My insides went warm. "Uh, Danny, I don't know about—"

"Sorry, no arguments. How about dinner tonight. What time should I pick you up?"

My throat tightened. I glanced at my phone. No text back from Aiden, but maybe he'd answer…warring emotions piled on top of me like a suffocating blanket.

"I have to meet Derek later. We'll see."

* * *

A snooty maître de led Derek and me to a table by the window in an overly-trendy bistro in Studio City. Now this was my idea of eating out. I took the cloth napkin off my bread plate and laid it across my lap.

Derek frowned at the sparkling silverware, the pristine tablecloth, and the small chandelier above our table.

I knew this place would drive him nuts. It was the reason I'd picked it even if I did admit that the food wasn't any better than his taco joint.

A waiter in traditional black pants and white, button-down shirt took our order then walked off with a slight nod.

Derek rolled his eyes and sipped water from his glass goblet. Then he straightened the salt and pepper shaker, rubbed his fingers along the rim of a vase of real daisies, and finally picked up a roll from the basket. After reaching for a pat of butter and lifting his knife he said, "We definitely have different taste, James."

I ignored his comment. "So, how was Palm Springs?"

Derek froze, buttered roll halfway to his mouth. "You knew where I was?"

"Not at first. But after I put Maya on it, she had your whole trip itinerary in minutes. I even know what you had for breakfast yesterday."

Derek grinned. "Damn, I underestimated you, kid."

"Not bad for a bunch of chicks, huh?"

"Not bad, period," he amended.

"So, spill it. What were you doing in Palm Springs? Because I swear to God if you were cheating on Elaine..."

"Jesus, James, I wasn't cheating on her. Where do you get the idea that every guy is a cheat?"

I raised a get-real eyebrow at him.

"Never mind," he said, waving off the obvious answer that growing up in the backseat of his Bonneville on stake-outs might have skewed my idea on relationships just a tad. "All right, you wanna know the truth?" he asked, setting down his roll.

"Please."

"I was...at a doctor."

I froze. "Why? What's wrong?"

"Nothing. It's just a little...procedure I had done."

I felt my throat constrict, fear and visions of hospital beds after his shooting flashing back to me. "What kind of procedure?"

"It was nothing," he said, averting my eyes.

"What. Kind," I pressed, converting my paralyzing fear into anger instead.

Derek sighed. "Surgery. Okay? Prostate surgery."

I blinked at him. "God, Derek, why didn't you tell me? Are you okay? Is it..." I trailed off, not able to say the "C" word out loud.

Luckily, he read my mind. "No, no, nothing like that. Just a little...enlarged," he mumbled, fiddling with his roll. "Look I didn't want you to worry. Dr. Murphy at Palm Medical is the best. He says I'll be back to new in no time."

"Why didn't you tell Elaine?"

"Look, it's embarrassing."

"Seriously? What are you, twelve?"

He bit his lip. "It's...well, an enlarged prostate can sometimes make it hard to get the little soldier into battle..."

"Stop!" I said, putting my hand up. "TMI."

"Anyway, that's why I went into the doc in the first place, and he ran some tests and they wanted to do treatment. But I'm fine. I take it easy for a few days, and I'm good as new."

"You sure?" I pressed, knowing full well I intended to have Maya hack into his medical records later and make sure the old geezer was telling me the truth this time.

"Positive," he reassured me. "Doc says my little soldier should be ready for battle in no time."

I rolled my eyes. "You need to tell Elaine."

He grew silent for a moment, then finally nodded. "How's she doing?"

"Okay. She had a few rough patches, afraid of what you were up to." I didn't need to tell him I felt the same way. "But we talked, bonded. She's a great lady."

He smiled. "I told you."

Now that I knew he wasn't cheating, I couldn't help but wonder what this meant for the two of them. Would I one day refer to Elaine as my step-mom? Was Derek possible of committing to one woman?

"Hey, you got dinner plans tonight?" he asked. "Thought maybe you'd want to spend some time on the boat with your old man?"

I opened my mouth to answer when my phone rang.

I paused. Was it Aiden? Danny? And who did I want it to be?

Instead of checking, I reached down and shut off the phone, mid-ring. Then I smiled up at Derek. "I'm all yours, Dad."

ABOUT THE AUTHORS

Gemma Halliday is the *New York Times* and *USA Today* bestselling author of the *High Heels Mysteries*, the *Hollywood Headlines Mysteries,* the *Jamie Bond Mysteries,* and several other works. Gemma's books have received numerous awards, including a Golden Heart, two National Reader's Choice awards, and three RITA nominations. She currently lives in the San Francisco Bay Area where she is hard at work on several new projects.

To learn more about Gemma, visit her online at
www.GemmaHalliday.com

Jennifer Fischetto, national bestselling author, writes dead bodies for ages thirteen to six-feet-under. When not writing, she enjoys reading, eating, singing, and watching way too much TV. She also adores trees, thunderstorms, and horror movies. She lives in Western Massachusetts with her two awesome children, who love to throw new ideas her way, and two fuzzy cats, who love to get in the way.

For more information, follow her on Twitter:
@jennfischetto or visit her at http://jenniferfischetto.com.

Enjoyed this book? Check out these other fun reads available in print now from
Gemma Halliday Publishing:

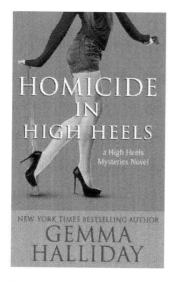

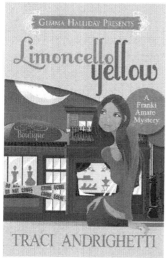

www.GemmaHalliday.com/Halliday_Publishing

Made in the USA
Middletown, DE
21 February 2016